ALSO BY CAROLINE B. COONEY:

The Face on the Milk Carton
Whatever Happened to Janie?
Both Sides of Time
Out of Time
Driver's Ed
Twenty Pageants Later
Among Friends
Camp Girl-Meets-Boy
Camp Reunion
Family Reunion
Operation: Homefront

THE
VOICE
ON THE
RADIO

CAROLINE B. COONEY

DELACORTE PRESS

Published by
Delacorte Press
Bantam Doubleday Dell Publishing Group, Inc.
1540 Broadway
New York, New York 10036

Library of Congress Cataloging-in-Publication Data
Cooney, Caroline B.
    The voice on the radio / Caroline B. Cooney.
        p.   cm.
    Companion novel to The face on the milk carton and Whatever happened to Janie?
    Summary: Sixteen-year-old Janie feels devastated when she discovers that her boyfriend has betrayed her and her family through his college radio program.
    ISBN 0-385-32213-5 (alk. paper)
    [1. Friendship—Fiction.   2. Parent and child—Fiction.
3. Brothers and sisters—Fiction.]   I. Title.
PZ7.C7834Vo   1996
[Fic]—dc20   96-3688
                                                                CIP
                                                                AC

The text of this book is set in 11-point Bookman.

Manufactured in the United States of America

October 1996

10   9   8   7   6   5   4   3   2

for Harold,
who knew what happened to Reeve

and with thanks to Lynne Hawkins, a
great line editor

to Sayre, whose idea of editing is "Wow, Mom,
this is perfect!"

and to Beverly Horowitz, my editor,
whose ideas are perfect

CHAPTER
ONE

FROM: JanieJson@aol.com
TO: ReeveShlds@hills.edu
SUBJ: unfair ccalendar practices rfor
studentsc
You have been at college 39 days = how
have i survived without you? Not easily. Why do i need high school? 599
days before i graduate. Come get me — i
have THSD . . . terminal high school
disease. Only cure = you. looooooove
janie

ReeveShlds@hills.edu
JanieJson@aol.com
h.s. diploma
Necessary 4 you to pay full price of
high school like every other American.
remember that 599 days is really only
19 monthys, which is a very low number.
cannot come and get you til I am rich
and famous, which is soon . . . in ONE
HOURr . . . thats 1 hour . . . I, yours
truly, will be a real live dj on a real
live radio station . . . Reeve

• • •

He ran out of things to say.

Reeve had never expected to have mike fright.

How could he have run out of things to talk about?

Eleven minutes into the hour for which he had begged and pleaded, and he was about to blow it. His tongue was drying out. Another sixty seconds and he wouldn't even be able to make sounds.

Reeve felt he could go to war in the jungle and not be scared. Be a cop at night in the projects during a drug war and not be scared. He was in a radio station with a mike at his mouth and nothing to say, and he was scared.

Dead air. You could kill a lot of things in a big city and nobody would look up, but people don't stayed tuned to dead air. Dead air is a dead jock.

Derek Himself, an experienced deejay, was sitting in one of those office chairs that bend backward, so he was grinning at the ceiling, flopping his right hand toward Reeve, planning to take back the mike.

Reeve grabbed himself a safety zone. "This is WSCK, We're Here, We're Yours, We're Sick! Coming to you live from the basement of your very own administration building. Now let's hear a brand-new release from Visionary Assassins, a Revere Dorm band."

Visionary Assassins were three guys who hadn't known each other when college began on August twenty-seventh, but now, October fourth, they had a band and a demo tape and wanted to be famous,

3

respected and rich, performing live to packed, adoring audiences nationwide.

Reeve had loved radio all his life: talk shows and call-in shows, hard rock and soft rock, country and western and acid rock—anything except Easy Listening. He could even stand the two-hour news programming his parents liked at dinnertime, and now and then, for laughs, he'd tune in the local station—lost dog descriptions and advertising so pathetic he was embarrassed.

But he had never thought of being a jock himself.

Radio was so completely a thing for the car or the house that it never occurred to Reeve that radio could be *him*.

He had walked into the studio of WSCK only because the freshman dorm made him nervous: fifteen hundred college students he didn't know. How did you find a life among so many strangers? His roommate gave him the creeps. Reeve could not believe he was going to have to share a ten-by-twelve cubbyhole with this animal for nine months. Cordell didn't brush his teeth, didn't wash his underwear, didn't plan to change his sheets. It was a stage, Cordell said proudly. Well, move on to a better one, said Reeve, who was inviting smokers to drop by in order to cover the odor of his roommate.

How Hills College had ever admitted Cordell was a mystery. An even greater mystery was that girls were flirty with Cordell.

But after just one night volunteering on the college radio station, roommate problems became too minor to bother with.

4

Reeve knew what he wanted in this world: the sound of his own voice on the air. People listening to him. People saying Hey, shut up, everybody, Reeve Shields is coming on.

Of course he wasn't using his last name. He wanted to be one of those few people on earth for whom one name is plenty. Reeve.

And here he was: so scared he was in danger of forgetting his name, never mind making it immortal.

Inside the headphones, Reeve listened to Visionary Assassins. The music was so live. The drumbeats meshed with Reeve's pulse, and the bass thrummed in his heart. The headphones were extremely good: soft and easy to wear, no sense of weight or pressure. Just complete enclosure within strong, hot sound.

Unfortunately, this was supposed to be a provocative talk hour, not a music hour.

Derek Himself smiled an I-told-you-so smile. Derek had a purple Mohawk, seven earrings in one ear and three in the other. "Hey, honey," he said, "want me to take over for you?"

"I'm fine," said Reeve, smiling falsely. One dark night, he would ambush and mutilate Derek for calling him honey.

Through most of his life, Reeve had had one goal: to top six feet. Having done that, he had yearned for muscles. Having acquired those, he had been willing to consider studying. By that time, it was his senior year in high school. It was kind of a kick to get A instead of C minus. Reeve had had every intention of studying at college, too. Studying was cool. It was him, it was good, it was the whole point behind his parents' forking over tens of thousands of dollars.

When he had wandered into WSCK, though, that had been it for studying.

Now—all six feet of Reeve looking at all five-five of Derek—Reeve understood that muscles and strength were meaningless on radio. Ability to go on talking was what counted. Broad shoulders were not going to rescue him.

"Think of a topic you can run with," said Derek. "Maybe you'll be lucky and some creep will call in and you can get mileage out of a sick phone call. Or maybe you'll be so boring that a normal person will call in and ask you to yield the mike to Derek Himself."

This was Derek's name on the air: Derek Himself. Derek managed these two words as if he were introducing the President of the United States.

Visionary Assassins unfortunately had a short opening song. It ended.

Reeve had forty-six minutes to fill and nothing to say.

• • •

Janie and Sarah-Charlotte sat on Janie's bed studying brides' magazines. They had split the cost of two new ones. Sarah-Charlotte, who was very practical, read the articles on joint checking accounts. Janie, who detested practicality, looked at gowns.

"Your marriage will never last," observed Sarah-Charlotte, "because you're too romantic. The only reason you'd get married is to wear a long white dress. Remember, you only get to wear the dress for a few hours."

"Who asked you?" said Janie. "Anyway, if I marry Reeve, he's a romantic too."

"Wouldn't that be fun?" said Sarah-Charlotte. "I can just see Reeve waiting for you at the altar."

So could Janie. Ever since senior prom, the first and only time she had seen Reeve in a tuxedo, she had had wedding dreams. The crisp black and white, the formal tension of starch and cuffs—she could transfer whole hours of prom memory into her future wedding.

Of course, she didn't tell Reeve about this. She was a high-school junior and Reeve a college freshman. If Janie said "wedding" out loud, he'd probably buy a sailboat and circumnavigate the globe for a decade or two.

There was no stopping a Reeve fantasy once it took off. Now Janie saw herself keeping house on a yacht.

Sarah-Charlotte studied flower arrangements for modern brides. "Janie, which of your fathers would walk you down the aisle?"

This was a serious problem. Janie considered Daddy her father, of course; and he was; he had brought her up. But there was also her New Jersey dad, of whom she was becoming quite fond. "I could have both of them," she said. "One on each arm."

"Yikes! Would they do that for you?"

"Sure," said Janie. Could I do that to them? she thought. It would be so hard on them both. Of course, I've done everything else to them—why flinch now?

"But," said Sarah-Charlotte, who had learned to ask for details without a question, "everything should be settling down now."

She'll probably be a reporter, thought Janie, getting silent people to talk by saying something they have to contradict. "I don't think things ever settle down in this kind of situation," said Janie. "It's like an extra-extra-extra-extra-wicked divorce."

"I don't know if it's four-extra," said Sarah-Charlotte. "Two-extra, tops."

They heard Janie's mother on the stairs, tucked the brides' magazines under the bed and began a loud, pointless discussion about chemistry assignments. Mrs. Johnson went into her own room and, moments later, ran back downstairs.

"I don't know why we act as if we're doing something bad," said Sarah-Charlotte, retrieving the magazines. "Every normal girl dreams of her wedding day."

"We're supposed to be reading investment magazines so we can plan our Wall Street careers, or computer magazines so we can plan our high-tech careers," agreed Janie, "when all we want to do is design our wedding invitations."

They designed a wedding invitation. How pleasingly the names *Reeve Shields* and *Jane Elizabeth Johnson* rested on the page.

"You'll have to get married under your real name, you know," said Sarah-Charlotte. "Otherwise it won't be legal." Sarah-Charlotte wrote another wedding invitation.

Reeve Shields and *Jennie Spring.*

The name *Jennie Spring* still made Janie queasy. She felt that she had barely escaped demolition; she was a building that had been scheduled to be blown up. The switch was still there, and *Jennie Spring* was still an explosive device.

Janie changed the subject. "Let's do one for you, Sarah-Charlotte." Janie drew a rectangle for another wedding invitation. "You still have a crush on Alec, don't you?"

"Yes, but not on wedding invitations. His last name is too hideous. Kinkle. Ugh. He's going to have to take my name instead."

"Sarah-Charlotte Kinkle. I don't know, it has kind of an interesting sound. Nobody would forget you."

Sarah-Charlotte was insulted. "I will have such a spectacular career that nobody will forget me anyhow."

"Cool. What will you do?"

"I don't know yet, but I'll do it better than anybody." Sarah-Charlotte turned to the beginning of the magazine and studied the masthead. "Editor-in-chief," she said. "That's a possibility. I'll put out a magazine so startling it will change the wedding world."

Janie giggled. "I don't think brides want to be startled." Janie would have been happy to stay on frothy subjects, but Sarah-Charlotte, of course, got sick of it, stopped being subtle and said, "So what exactly is happening in New Jersey, Janie?"

New Jersey was code for the Other Family. The Biological Family. The Springs.

The Springs had actually visited Janie, in this

very house. Well, the kids, of course, not the parents. The parents she had dumped were not ready to visit the parents she preferred. But Stephen, Jodie and the twins had come twice. Amazingly, her Spring brothers and sister seemed peaceful about the two families.

"What do you mean—*exactly*?" said Janie grumpily. "Nobody ever knows anything *exactly*."

"Okay, start here. Are they getting better about it?"

Everybody said *it*. Nobody called *it* by any other name because *it* was too crazy and complicated. Janie said not only *it* but also *them* because she did not know what to call her other family. A person with two sets of parents, one of whom had been involved in kidnapping her, had trouble constructing sentences.

Janie could never talk about *it*. When Sarah-Charlotte brought *it* up over and over again, so bluntly, insisting that the best friend deserved the most gossip, Janie wanted to scream, or else go attend college with Reeve. She couldn't stand how *it* never closed up, never went away, but was always in front of her, like fresh tar she'd step in and her life would stick.

Janie felt herself turning into a paper doll again. As a paper doll, she could keep her smile out front and her agony flat and hidden on the back.

This was the sort of thing you did not say to any adult. Adults were quick to leap off their chairs and out of their minds and force you once more to go to counseling.

This is my best friend! she thought. And I feel as if she's a police officer interrogating me.

Janie had learned, this year, to take questions in her hands and bend them off to the side. "I guess New Jersey doesn't matter as much as Boston," she said.

Boston meaning Reeve. Boston meaning boyfriends.

Oh, Reeve! thought Janie. If only you were here! I'm under siege from my own best friend, who won't give it a rest.

The stab of Reeve gone was like a medieval spear; an iron lance leaving a hole in her life. She didn't want him crisp and starched in a tuxedo, but soft in cords and his old fleece jacket. The part of his anatomy she wanted most was his shoulder, where she used to tuck herself in, and close her eyes, and let Reeve decide what happened next. Sometimes she wanted to go next door to Reeve's house, steal his old jacket, and have it to hold.

"He still faxing you every day?" said Sarah-Charlotte.

"It's slacked off a little. And sometimes it's telephone or e-mail or a Hallmark card."

But none of that helped much. Reeve just plain wasn't here. He lived in a dorm she had never seen, had friends with whom she had never spoken, had a new wardrobe she had never seen him wear.

When Janie and Reeve got together, they didn't talk about it because it was old stuff for them. Been there, done it, seen it. With Reeve, Janie was no paper doll. Best of all, she was not Jennie Spring, explosive device.

She drew a necklace of hearts around the wedding invitation that said *Jane Elizabeth Johnson.*

11

There was nothing she had not shared with Reeve.

Well, within reason. She had not shared with Reeve her hobby of drawing up their wedding invitations. She aimed for the new yacht fantasy and tried to step aboard, tried to stand on the teak deck and hear the wind whipping in the sails.

"Ooooh, here's a great maid-of-honor gown!" squealed Sarah-Charlotte. "Dark wine-red velvet. Perfect for a winter wedding. Just my color."

"It's a beautiful gown," Janie agreed. Sarah-Charlotte's white-blond hair would look like its own veil against that deep wine red.

But I have a sister now, thought Janie. A sister with auburn-red hair like mine. Isn't your sister supposed to be your maid of honor? And Jodie would look better in green. How do I tell Sarah-Charlotte she can't be my maid of honor? How do I sort out the fathers of the bride?

It's just as well that Reeve doesn't know about the wedding, she thought. I'm not quite ready myself.

She ached for Reeve. It was physical, that ache, located inside her arms. She needed to curve around him.

•　•　•

Think of a topic! Reeve yelled at himself.

His mind was a clear space.

Politics? He didn't know anything.

The world? Nobody on campus cared.

Music? He couldn't think of the name of a single band on the face of the earth.

Nature? Women's rights? Traffic jams?

What do people talk about on the air? thought Reeve.

His mind was as smooth as the polish on a new car. His brain was buffed. The microphone was waiting; Derek was laughing silently and gladly.

Reeve had been a deejay for the first time from three A.M. to four A.M.—an hour when even college kids slept and the number of listeners probably hovered around two. It came easily: no clenching up, no fumbling for words, no mispronunciations. After two weeks at three A.M., Reeve had talked his way into prime time.

Derek's advice had been against Reeve, and Derek was about to be proved correct.

Reeve had told everybody. Two of his classes were lectures with five hundred strangers. When the prof asked for questions at the end of class, Reeve stood up and announced his broadcast hour. His other two classes had twenty-five kids, and he'd told them, and of course he'd told the guys on his dorm floor and the girls on the floor below—people he had to live with.

Why, oh why, hadn't he chickened out? Every single person he would ever know at Hills College was going to hear him being a jerk and a loser.

Of course, they might not be listening.

It was just a college station. They were probably listening to real stations.

If I fail, it's okay, he told himself. Nobody but me cares, and it's no big deal, and—

If he failed, he would transfer to another college.

It would be fun asking his parents for another ten or twenty thousand dollars in order for their son not to be humiliated on the air.

It's nothing but a microphone, he said to himself. Say something. Say anything. "Once upon a time," said Reeve.

Derek Himself stared incredulously. Cal, a deejay, and Vinnie, the station manager, who were the other two guys at the station tonight, looked up from their paperwork. All three began to snicker, and then actually to snort, with laughter, although background noise was forbidden when the mike was on; it would be picked up and broadcast. *Once upon a time?* A beginning for kindergartners. A beginning for fairy tales and picture books.

Reeve would never live it down. He really would have to transfer.

He pictured Cordell laughing at him. Laughed at by a roommate stupider and smellier than anybody on campus? He imagined the guys in the dorm yelling *Loser! Loser!* Guys he wanted to be friends with but hadn't pulled it off yet. Guys who would not be polite about how worthless Reeve was.

"Once upon a time," he repeated helplessly, stuck in horrible repetition of that stupid phrase.

And then talk arrived, like a tape that had come in the mail. For Reeve Shields really did know a story that began with "Once upon a time."

"I dated a dizzy redhead. Dizzy is a compliment. Janie was light and airy. Like hope and joy. My girlfriend," he said softly, into the microphone. Into the world.

"You know the type. Really cute, fabulous red hair, lived next door. Good in school, of course, girls like that always are. Janie had lots of friends

14

and she was crazy about her mom and dad, because that's the kind of family people like that have."

Never had Reeve's voice sounded so rich and appealing.

"Except," said Reeve, "except one day in the school cafeteria, a perfectly ordinary day, when kids were stealing each other's desserts and spilling each other's milk, Janie just happened to glance down at the picture of that missing child printed on the milk carton."

His slow voice seemed to draw a half-pint of milk, with its little black-and-white picture of a missing child. It was almost visible, that little milk carton, that dim and wax-covered photograph.

"And the face on the milk carton," said Reeve, "was Janie herself."

He deepened his voice, moving from informative into mysterious. "They can't fit much information on the side of a half-pint," said Reeve, "but the milk carton said that little girl had been missing since she was three. Missing for twelve years."

In radio, you could not see your audience. Reeve could not know whether he really did have an audience. Radio was faith.

"Can you imagine if your daughter, or your sister, had disappeared twelve years ago? Twelve years have gone by, and yet you still believe. Surely somehow, somewhere, she must be waiting, and listening. You haven't given up hope. You refuse to admit she's probably dead by now, probably was dead all along. You believe there is a chance in a million that if you put her picture on a milk carton, she'll see it."

15

Beyond the mike, Reeve imagined dormitories—kids slouched on beds and floors, listening. Listening to him.

"Well," said Reeve, "she saw it."

• • •

To Jodie, the space of the big, new house was incredible. Only a year ago, especially during that brief, terrifying time when Janie lived with them, there had been five kids and their friends. The little split-level had been jammed with kids: kids on the couch, kids on the floor, kids in the refrigerator, kids spending the night, kids practicing the clarinet, kids throwing balls, kids fighting, millions of kids.

Now there was a big, clean, empty space with Jodie rattling around.

The new house was such a good idea. What color wallpaper should go in the twins' bathroom? Should there be sliding doors to the deck or French doors? Jodie's parents got very involved. Paint chips became a major part of their lives, and of course, no matter what you decide on paint, and whether lemon yellow turns out to be right or wrong, it's only paint. Paint it again if you goofed.

After Janie, it was pretty decent to have things you could just paint over when you were wrong.

Jodie's brother Stephen was at college for the house event. Everybody on the East Coast had to go through a Colorado stage, and Stephen was deep in his, happy to have Birkenstocks on his feet and mountains in his backyard.

Not only was Stephen gone, but nobody really noticed. It was natural and easy to have him out of the family. Whereas when Jennie had left to become Janie again, it had been unnatural and terrible and it had ruined their sleep and their eating and their lives.

So last year there had been five Spring children, and then Jennie had left and there were four, and then Stephen had left and there were three.

The twins had been thick and annoying all their paired lives, and they simply continued. There was no need to think about Brian and Brendan because they had each other and did enough thinking between them.

Jodie felt as if she were the only child. It was quite wonderful. Mom consulted her over everything: carpet swatches and the locations of electrical outlets and the colors of bathroom sinks. Mom and Dad were so tickled, bursting out of the old, cramped place. They had refused to change addresses or phone numbers after the kidnapping, even when a decade had passed and missing three-year-old Jennie was unquestionably dead and gone.

But Jodie's parents had questioned. They had put their little girl's picture on a milk carton, and the right little girl had seen it.

After all these months, it could still chill Jodie's bones that Janie Johnson had seen herself on a milk carton and had understood that she must be Jennie Spring.

Jodie put aside her shattered hopes for a sister, the one whose name would match and who would be as close to her as a twin, and considered college instead.

Stephen, now—her brother Stephen had always

known he would leave; leave for good; put hundreds of miles between himself and this family. Jodie was not sure she could do that. She felt that her mother and father needed her more than they had needed Stephen. Or perhaps it was different for sons; perhaps parents yielded their sons more easily.

But Jodie was the only daughter—Janie having quit—and Mom and Dad were frightened when she looked through college catalogs from California or Texas or Michigan. There weren't many schools in New Jersey and if the college experience was going to count, Jodie at least needed to get out of state. So she was looking in New York and Pennsylvania. Connecticut she would skip, because *Connecticut* was the Spring family word for kidnap and loss and rage. That brought her eyes up the map to Rhode Island and Massachusetts. If she went to school in Providence or Boston, she'd be on the railroad line and could get home easily. Nobody would have to rearrange a life to come get her in the car.

It was autumn.

The time, for high school seniors, of looking at college campuses. Jodie Spring looked at the catalog for Hills College, and she thought, Janie's boyfriend goes there. He'd show me around the campus. It would be cool to see Boston with Reeve.

•　•　•

Were Derek Himself, Vinnie and Cal into his story? Had he pulled it off? Reeve didn't risk looking at them. If they were laughing at him . . .

Reeve had found a beat. He felt instinctively that

18

Janie's story must be told slowly, in a rhythm of confusing omissions, so that people wanted more. It had to be the same puzzling nightmare that it had been for Janie.

"So it's *you* on that milk carton. *You are a missing person*," breathed Reeve.

The mike ate his words, hungered for more.

"Around you, everything is ordinary. People are still having Jell-O and sitting two to a chair. But your life just switched channels."

Now Reeve's mind was crammed with a whole library of radio time. Janie Johnson was a story to tell forever.

"What does *missing* mean?" asked Reeve. His eyes were fixed on the fat, gray mike. His fingers teased the adjustable arm, making friends with it, getting safe. "Does *missing* mean *lost*? Does it mean *run away*? Or does it mean . . . *kidnapped*?"

Janie and her two families had never given interviews.

Not once.

Not to anybody.

Reeve, and Reeve alone, knew both sides completely; knew more than Janie, really, because his parents had talked to Janie's parents and to the police, back when Janie was still too horrified to hear or see or listen.

"Of course," said Reeve, dragging his voice like a net to catch listeners, "the question is—*now what?* Because you love your parents. If you tell anybody you think you were kidnapped, well—think about it. Think about the media. The police. Your family would be destroyed. If these grown-ups you call

Mommy and Daddy are really your kidnappers, and if you turn them in, you'll send your own parents to prison."

Two beats of silence. Then a lowering of the voice. "But if you don't tell . . . *what about that other family?* Still out there? Still worrying, after all these years?"

Derek was staring, a pencil dangling in his hand. Vinnie's mouth was half open, like a little kid at story hour. Cal was tilting back apprehensively, to get away from the idea that the family you love must have kidnapped you.

I have an audience, thought Reeve.

It was a hot, winning feel: like hitting the ball out of the stadium when the bases were loaded.

I can do this, thought Reeve. I'm good at it.

To the audience he could not see—might not even have—he repeated, *"Now what?"*

CHAPTER
TWO

Sarah-Charlotte needed to know exactly what wardrobe Janie was taking for her next visit back to New Jersey.

"It doesn't matter," Janie pointed out. She didn't feel like discussing the impending visit, especially because she wasn't going down there; they were coming here. With Sarah-Charlotte, Janie would find herself creating and keeping secrets there was no point in having. "I've gone back before," she told Sarah-Charlotte carelessly, "they're used to me, and anyway, they know my whole wardrobe from when I lived there, so it's no big deal."

"Clothing is always a big deal," said Sarah-Charlotte crossly. "Don't tell me you're becoming one of these annoying people who pretends fashion doesn't matter."

Janie giggled. It was an all-purpose, change-the-subject giggle. "You know what? I care so much about fashion I just bought a new Barbie I didn't have."

Janie flung herself over the edge of the bed, and Sarah-Charlotte held her ankles while Janie groped around under the starched lace skirt. She yanked on the handle of her Barbie suitcase. They sprung the locks and took out the new purchase. Barbie on a High Stepper Horse. A palomino with even better hair than Barbie. Janie began to braid the horse's hair.

"When I was eight, I would have killed for this," said Sarah-Charlotte. She picked out the flexible gymnastics Barbie and began to dress her as a Pizza Hut waitress. "Why don't you go visit Reeve?" she said. "Wouldn't it be fun to stay in his dorm?"

Janie was feeling flimsy. She did not want to talk about Reeve. Boston seemed as distant as Tibet, and the college life that Reeve led as strange and unknown as the Himalayas. "*My* parents? Allow me to travel to Boston and stay in a boys' dorm? Get a grip on yourself, Sarah-Charlotte."

They both laughed. Janie's parents, and of course "them," in New Jersey, didn't let anybody do anything. Not with their history.

"Get Reeve to drive down," said Sarah-Charlotte. "Just for an afternoon, anyway."

She knows how much I miss him, thought Janie. I've kept it from her, but she knows that even when Reeve couldn't find the right words to solve things, he always had the right arms and the right shoulders. "He doesn't have a car," she said. "It's Boston. What would he do with a car? He'd have to park it, which is impossible, and repair it when it gets broken into."

Sarah-Charlotte nodded, letting Janie escape the subject of Reeve. "I had higher hopes for Barbie than being a waitress. I expected her to be an airline pilot. Barbie," said Sarah-Charlotte sadly, "how did you slip to this?"

She really is my best friend, thought Janie.
Friend. The word seemed like Barbie: warm and tan and always the same. I wonder, thought Janie, if it's too late to be friends with my sister, Jodie.

• • •

WSCK was a music station, but it didn't try to compete with commercial Boston stations. There was no point in featuring somebody from the eighties, like John Cougar Mellencamp, or somebody who would last forever, like Aerosmith. They didn't wrestle with how close to Pearl Jam they should play Stone Temple Pilots (since those bands sounded exactly the same except different). They didn't worry about whether to have a jazz hour, or whether to expand their reggae and rap.

WSCK did garage bands. Local bands. Hopefuls trying desperately to climb past unadvertised evenings in unknown clubs. Mostly, they did college dorm bands.

Boston was full of colleges. Northeastern, Simmons, Boston College, Boston University, New England Conservatory, Wentworth, and Reeve's college, Hills. Just across the bridge were Harvard and MIT. Two hundred and fifty thousand college kids in Boston, and on every floor of every dorm were kids who wanted to make it as musicians.

All of them needed airtime. Bands walked constantly through the doors of WSCK, holding out their homemade tapes or CDs or even records; amazingly enough, people were still cutting records. Reeve loved the smell of vinyl. He loved the musicians, whether they were garage bands or just garbage. They tried so hard. They were so brave and willing to be humiliated, as long as they got heard.

The playlist at WSCK was not a computer-generated work of art. No research team was finding out if the listening audience on Huntington Avenue wanted more or less Melissa Etheridge. Nobody cared about Melissa Etheridge. They cared about themselves.

Only at ten P.M. did the format change.

From ten to eleven, the station featured talk. Sometimes it was right-wing, sometimes left-wing. Sometimes it was hate, sometimes it was New Age love. It was opinion on legalizing marijuana. Or opinion on retiring all current professors at all currently existing universities. (People were in favor.)

But mostly, it was the radio jocks themselves. Teenagers who wanted talk shows. Jocks who wanted to go back to their home states and do the wildly sick and funny and famous morning shows for commuters in Los Angeles or Chicago or Miami. Jocks who wanted to make it with their speaking voices, just as the bands wanted to make it with their songs and drumbeats.

Reeve thought: I'll be the next talk-show king.

He loved the vision of himself—famous and surrounded by admirers and sought after by other famous people. He could hardly wait to listen to the tape of himself after his hour was done.

Janie didn't tell. She kept it a secret between herself and the milk carton.

Janie researched her own kidnapping in The
New York Times.

*Can you imagine? You go to the library and
read about yourself on microfiche? You see
a photograph in the* Times *of a sister and
three brothers you never knew you had? An
uncle and an aunt and grandparents . . .
but most of all, a mother and father?*

But even The New York Times *doesn't know
who took you. They only know the family
that got left behind. The FBI, the Jersey police, nobody ever had a clue.*

*But you know. It has to be the parents you
have right now.*

Radio is partly about phone calls. Would anybody call in? Would even two or three people
bother?

The part of Reeve that was conscious of anything beyond the mike was conscious of the phone.

Please, let it ring. Let it prove people are listening to me.

---

*Trouble is, your parents are good, nice, re-
sponsible people. And you love them. Kidnapping is evil. Does this mean the mother
and father you love are evil?*

*If you go and telephone that 800 number on
that milk carton, hey—it's finished. Over.
You lose. No more family.*

So you try to figure out a way that you could

25

be wrong. That it's made up. That the face
on the milk carton is not you.
But you start finding proof.
Like a box. In an attic. Under the eaves.

•   •   •

Brian Spring and his mother were still at Price
Club. Mom's workdays were long, and by the time
dinner was over, and homework supervised, and
she could think of shopping, it was always late. In
their new Dodge Caravan, they had headed out to
stockpile food and drink and plastic bags and de-
tergents.

When the twins were little (actually, a year ago),
both Brendan and Brian loved shopping days. The
huge warehouse was as awesome as an airplane
hangar, with checkouts like tollbooths. You bought
vast quantities of food—a case of hot dogs, econo-
packs of towels, a gallon of Wesson Oil.

Now Brendan scorned shopping. Brendan had
better things to do. Along with the soccer team,
he'd added weight lifting and swimming, so that he
could become one of those guys who are scary before they're even out of junior high. He was planning to shave his head and get a tattoo.

For thirteen years the two boys had been sealed
up like an envelope. They had lived in synchrony,
without effort or bickering.

But now Brendan was a sports star and Brian
hadn't even made the team. Brendan was quick to
accuse people, including his twin, of being a girl.
There was nothing worse than somebody who

26

threw like a girl, or ran like a girl. When Mom asked who wanted to go shopping, Brendan said, "*Shopping!* That's for *girls.*" He gave Brian his look of contempt reserved for people who were girls.

Jodie also refused to go shopping. She had college catalogs to study.

So Brian had to go because his mother looked lost.

It was during shopping that they had lost Janie all those years ago. Whenever she took the remaining four children shopping, their mother was a dog trainer, her children on mental and eyeball leashes. You did not scout out a different display, because kidnappers might lurk only an aisle away.

But they were too old for that now. If somebody rotten appeared, they'd just whap the kidnapper with a gallon of applesauce.

Now Mom was the one who was lost. Mom was trying to get her bearings in a world that had changed as much for her as school had changed for Brian.

School this fall had ended Brian's twinny life.

Since he and Brendan were reflections of each other, Brian had studied and read not one minute more than his twin, which was pretty much zero minutes.

On his own in a new school, and on his own in the huge, new house, with a private room for the first time in his life, Brian found out that he and Brendan were twins only on the surface. While Brendan was off being a star, Brian found himself in an American history class with the best teacher he had ever had; the only teacher to whom he had ever really paid attention.

Brian found history astonishing and wonderful. He loved the conquistadors, the explorers of the Northwest Passage, the frontiersmen, the Indians who fought back.

Book bags were key.

People thought you were carrying extra sneakers. Nobody, including your twin, suspected that you had library books. Brendan, who thought reading was for geeks who hit balls like girls, did not know that his very own twin had fallen in love with information.

The Springs were not an academic family.

Mom and Dad expected their children to do well in school. Stephen did well because he wanted to get into a distant college. Jodie did well because she liked to come in first. Brendan did well because the school imposed standards on athletes.

Only Brian did well because he loved learning.

I didn't know that before, he thought. It took a room to myself to find out what I love.

Whenever Stephen telephoned, Brian wanted to tell his big brother everything. But no useful sentences came out of his mouth. He said things like "Hey, Steve, how's Colorado? You climbed any mountains yet?"

Stephen—who had wanted so much to be a different person with a different family—would be happy for him. Stephen referred to his twin brothers as wasps. Friendly, but ready to sting if anybody interfered with their twinny lives. Brian wanted to tell Stephen that he didn't have a twinny life anymore: He missed it terribly, it hurt him like knives, and yet he was glad it was gone. Like Janie, he thought.

28

But he told Stephen nothing, and in return Stephen told him nothing, and Brian thought: No fair.

Mom piloted an immense shopping cart down wide aisles at Price Club. It was shrink-wrap heaven. Brian wished he had invented shrink wrap. Toothpaste, tuna fish, paint cans—all secured with plastic wrap so strong it might have been fending off chunks of space debris.

And the new house had acres of storage, so nobody had to surrender precious closet space to ten-packs of paper towels. Mom could buy meat lockers of hamburger, a dozen boxes of Cheerios.

Brian thought of early settlers planting a few grains of corn in a hill, a few seeds of squash to encircle them. He thought of little boys fending off crows and rabbits, of mothers drying and storing that grain, of long winters without enough to eat.

His mother heaved an immense strip of plastic-jacketed barbecued ribs into the cart. His mother seemed a complete stranger to him, just as his twin now seemed a stranger. Like Janie, he thought again. I stand around watching strangers who are related to me. I love them, but who are they? And why?

His mother suddenly whipped around, eyes too wide, hands out.

"I'm here, Mom," he said reassuringly. "I'm right behind you."

His mother tried to laugh. Tried to act casual. "You don't have to stay with me, Bri. You can wander off and see what you turn up. Might be something special over in Hardware."

Brian's heart broke for his mother. All these years of restrictions and rules, of tension and anxi-

29

ety: that iron grip she had kept on her children
. . . she could let go.

She knew that. But her body's reactions weren't
trained to the new life yet.

It occurred to Brian that he and his twin had
been pushed so hard into sports because a sport
kept them in one place. When your children were
at baseball practice, you knew where they were.
You knew there was a coach keeping watch. You
could breathe.

We're going to become the family we should
have been, thought Brian.

A family that can let go, and have space, and not
whip around in stores, sick with fear.

●   ●   ●

Reeve felt as if he had reached another plane of
living, the kind people talked about on the talk
shows that weren't into sex or violence. A plane of
joy and light.

The mike was his; he was the mike.

The audience was his; he was theirs.

---

*The milk carton became Janie's blanket. She
used my penknife to slit it open, so she
could flatten it out. She carried it under the
clip in her blue-cloth three-ring binder. You
know the kind. Where you write in ballpoint
pen on the cover. After the milk carton, she
was still my dizzy redhead, but dizzy
meant stumbling and scared. If the milk
carton was right, she had been kidnapped
when she was three. Janie sort of moved*

30

deeper toward being a three-year-old, as if that way, she could understand. Maybe even remember. It was just a matter of time before she started sucking her thumb. Meantime, a flattened milk carton from Flower Dairy became her blankie.

Vinnie, Cal and Derek were motionless with listening.

"Well," said Reeve breezily, knowing the incredible pride that comes from owning an audience, "I really liked that number by Visionary Assassins, didn't you? Hey, Assassins! Revere is my dorm, too; come visit me. I've never met any assassins, let alone assassins with vision. Let's listen to another song from the Assassins."

•   •   •

The phone lit up at WSCK. Vinnie answered. Vinnie was a neoconservative who hated all ethnic groups, all causes and all man- and womankind. He made a perfect station manager, since he never worried about hurting anybody's feelings. Vinnie took four phone calls.

He looked happy, which was not like Vinnie.

Visionary Assassins shrieked on, their lyrics grim and their chords threatening.

The phone lit up again and again.

Vinnie said, "Reeve. The callers want more about Janie."

CHAPTER
THREE

All talk-ups were automatically recorded on a tape called the air check. It was a reel-to-reel tape, the big, old-fashioned kind you didn't think existed anymore.

Vinnie, Cal, Derek and Reeve played back Reeve's hour. With no music in between, it was much shorter than Reeve had expected.

His own voice sounded unfamiliar. He would not have known it was him. He felt uncomfortable, as if that voice were somebody else, using his words.

"You have a great radio voice," said Vinnie, who despised everybody and their voice. If Vinnie said Reeve had a great radio voice, it was true.

Reeve listened to his great radio voice saying that any minute now, Janie would start sucking her thumb.

Reeve had made that up.

It was a good line. Dramatic. But it wasn't true. Janie had not acted three. She had acted the way any stricken person would, trying to protect the parents she loved from the truth she feared.

Live, Reeve's words had felt quite literally airy. The airwaves were his; and the power and the voice were his also.

But now the words were not air. They were permanent. They were, like the name of the station, SCK.

For a moment Janie was there with him, in the comfort posture she liked, tight against his chest, her eyes closed inside his hug.

What would she think of this broadcast?

He felt as if air had entered his gut, not his lungs. It was a sick floater feeling, like a drowning person.

Oh, well, he thought, she'll never know. Next time I'll talk about baseball. I've followed the Red Sox my whole life, and this year they actually might not screw up, so there's lots to talk about.

Vinnie said, "When it sounded as if you were finished talking, Reeve, we got *thirty-nine calls* wanting more about Janie!" Vinnie slammed his fist against a flimsy desk. A row of cassettes toppled. High numbers made him joyful. "It's only your first night!"

Which certainly implied Reeve would get a second night.

A CD by the Fog was coming to a close. Derek Himself signaled for silence. Vinnie, Cal and Reeve moved into the hall so that they could talk. Reeve watched Derek through the glass walls.

Deejays adjusted the mike every time they spoke. The need to touch the mike and be sure of it was strong. Derek actually launched his body with each sentence; a tiny dive into the deep, cold waters of an audience. Derek could not sit when he was talking. Nervous energy kept him on his feet. Vivid expressions crossed his face, as if the audience were in the room.

An hour ago, Reeve had hated Derek. Now he

watched avidly, drinking up the techniques of someone who'd been doing this for a long time.

"Okay, now, tomorrow night, Reeve," said Vinnie, "same format. A little on Janie, some music, another taste of Janie."

"Or do you think," said Cal seriously, "that he should just be on two nights a week? Say, Tuesday, Thursday. We don't want the audience to overdose."

This is me they're talking about, thought Reeve.

"Kind of save it," Vinnie said, nodding, "keep 'em coming back."

I don't belong at three A.M. I'm prime-time.

The room where Derek was now Himself had been designed for quiet and calm: soft gray carpet coated not just the floors, but also the walls. You could not write on those walls, but you could pin. The wall carpet was carpeted itself with concert posters and sick jokes and photographs of those immortal jocks who had been suspended for foul language or disgusting suggestions.

Everybody wanted to get suspended at least once.

Reeve thought of the suspension Janie Johnson would give him if she knew about this. Janie was a private person. Many a counselor, social worker or friend had expected to gain Janie's trust, and had failed. "No," he said awkwardly, "I'd better not do it again. Thanks for giving me a chance, it was fun."

"What do you mean—it was fun? It was brilliant," said Vinnie. "Reeve, this is the break we need. I could get a real job if I turn this pathetic, worthless college station into something. Thirty-nine calls? And they weren't nut cases. They were listeners." He said the word *listener* reverently, because listeners were precious. "You'll do another janie tomorrow night." Vinnie said this as if it were a new noun; an object; a janie.

"I don't think Janie would like it," said Reeve.

"You didn't even change her name to protect the innocent?" said Cal. "Some boyfriend. Listen, Reeve, you got style. Style is rare. You been on the air once and already people recognize your style and they're calling in for more."

The word *style* hung nicely, like great clothes.

"How many people could start out 'Once upon a time' and make it work?" said Vinnie. "You had great timing. The way you segued into Visionary Assassins—the way you slowed down your speech at the creepy parts- -you're a natural, Reeve."

I'm a natural, thought Reeve.

Derek Himself put on a CD, turned off the mike and sagged back into his everyday person. Vinnie, Cal and Reeve entered the broadcast room again. Derek scribbled on the playlist taped above the control board, inserted a CD for the next song and checked to be sure he had it on the correct track.

"Come on," said Vinnie, laughing at Reeve in a good-friends, we're-all-in-this-together way, "we have a broadcast range measured in city blocks. She's not gonna hear you down in Connecticut. She's still in high school! She's probably thinking about algebra or something. Do another one. Who's it gonna hurt?"

Reeve was surprised, almost embarrassed, to find himself missing Janie painfully, as if he'd got his fingers caught in a slammed door. It had al-

35

ways been Janie who closed her eyes, but now Reeve's closed, and she was there, complete with color and heat and voice.

The final chords on the tape disappeared like the back of a parade. Derek became Derek Himself again, jumping into the mike, eyebrows up and earrings swaying, punching On/Offs, sliding sliders, attacking the gooseneck of the mike.

". . . winding up another loooooong commercial-free music sweep with Fast Liars!" shouted Derek Himself. "Singing their new recording! 'Choke Collar'!"

Reeve loved the names of bands. Visionary Assassins. The Fog. Fast Liars. What a great world music was.

"I lied," said Derek Himself into the mike. "There is no band called Fast Liars and no song called 'Choke Collar.' But there would be if I could sing and write."

This is so much fun, thought Reeve. These guys are so great. This is why I came to college.

"No, what's really coming up," said Derek Himself, "is what's hot, what's big, what youuuuuuu've been on the phone demanding from us. Heeere's Reeve! With another janie."

•   •   •

"Shall we look for a six-bedroom house," Stephen's father had said uncertainly, when they'd started house-shopping the previous June, "so if Janie ever comes back, she'll have her own room?"

How Stephen hated it when his father sounded uncertain. He hated it that they had given up calling her Jennie, and everybody had agreed that

36

Jennie really had vanished more than a decade ago and his sister was really and truly Janie Johnson. He hated Jennie for having been kidnapped, for forcing him to lead the most protected life in New Jersey. "If she ever comes back," Stephen had said, "I'd rather she slept in a coffin."

"Shut up," Jodie had said. "If Janie ever comes back, Dad, she can share with me. You know she won't come for more than a weekend, and my new room has plenty of space for two beds."

Jodie's old room had fit two beds, too, but Janie hadn't wanted hers.

The Springs had found and bought a house within days, because Mom had said, "I can't wait," and Stephen knew this was literally true. For twelve terrible years, Mom had waited for the return of her daughter, and she could not keep waiting. "What color do you want your room to be?" she had asked Stephen a dozen times.

"It doesn't matter, Mom. I'll be at college. Paint it anything."

His mother had been crushed. As always, this had crushed Stephen right back. "Actually, I like blue," he said at last. "Cobalt blue."

This was the blue of Mrs. Johnson's magnificent living room. Stephen hoped his mother would not realize this. How stunned Stephen and his brothers and sister were that first strange weekend when they went to Connecticut to visit Janie with her kidnap family. Planning to crash the visit, hoping to crash the Johnsons, they were bewildered to find they liked the Johnsons.

And Stephen liked Reeve, who lived next door to the Johnsons.

Stephen and Reeve were the same age, but Reeve was so much more independent and sophisticated. Reeve at eighteen was just plain older than Stephen at eighteen. Stephen held the kidnapping responsible. How was a guy supposed to grow up in a household where they held your hand every minute of your existence?

Reeve was Stephen's model. Stephen couldn't match Reeve for muscles; he wasn't built that way. He gave up hoping for Reeve's inches, too, because you didn't grow after eighteen. But last spring and this summer, miraculously, Stephen had shot up to six-three. His body finally matched the enormous freaky feet attached to his ankles.

It was difficult for Stephen to care about Jennie-Janie or paint chips when the mirror had to be moved higher up on the wall or else his face wouldn't show.

Reeve had driven Janie down for her last visit before Stephen left for college.

What a moment, when Reeve had first seen Stephen's new inches. Reeve's grin had covered his entire face, reminding Stephen of a panting golden retriever. "Wow, Stephen," Reeve had shouted, "like tall! Like basketball hoop! Like extra-long mattresses!" Reeve had shaken hands with Stephen.

Then came the countdown: four weeks, three weeks, two, one—gone. Takeoff. Airplane wheels leaving the ground, putting behind his family history.

Sure enough, out here in Colorado, Stephen was too long for the regular mattress in the dorm. They had ordered an extra-long bed for him, but it hadn't come, so Stephen slept with his feet hanging off the end of the bed. He had gotten used to the odd posture of not enough mattress, and he was pretty sure he had grown yet another inch, because doorways threatened his forehead.

Out here in Colorado, nobody had ever heard of the Spring family. Nobody remembered the media attention. Stephen Spring was nobody but another (very tall) freshman on another (very large) campus.

Nobody was holding his hand.

Nobody was terrified if he was five minutes late.

He had no mother's anguish to worry about, no father's pain.

Stephen loved to leave his dorm late at night, stand on the parched earth, and look up at the huge, starry sky. He would think: I'll never go home. I'm done. They'll make it without me.

I'm free.

•   •   •

"Have you decided what colors you want in your bedroom, Brendan?" asked their mother. She was happily putting away her Price Club booty. She loved stashing a year's supply of tuna fish.

"Mom," said Brendan, in his new how-can-I-possibly-be-patient-with-this-dumb-woman? mode, "only girls care about colors."

"How about you, Bri?" said Mom.

Brian wanted a room just like the dining room at Mr. and Mrs. Johnson's house in Connecticut. The house in which Janie lived was dramatic and intense. Big strips of window alternated with vivid indigo walls or smash-you-in-the-face blood red walls. Mrs. Johnson knew how to decorate, and Brian had never previously considered such a thing as decoration. Now he saw that his own house was not decorated, merely full of furniture and very lived-in.

He could not say to his mother, "The colors I like are Janie's mom's colors. Drive up to Connecticut, will you, check them out, match them perfectly."

Connecticut meant The Enemy.

And yet, from the first visit, they weren't the enemy anymore. And after that first visit, for Brian, although it was not right for Janie to prefer her kidnap family to her real family, it was okay.

So he said, "I like red, Mom," and to prevent her from choosing wallpaper with sailboats or ducks, he said, "Just red paint. Like a barn." He hoped his twin would not recognize where he got his color choice from.

"It's after eleven," said their father. "How come nobody's in bed yet?"

Brian grinned up at his father. Brian remained a child in height and weight, the only Spring who was still little: The rest, including his very own twin, were tall. Brian wanted to talk about history, not bedtime or red paint or soccer. Nobody in this household cared.

It was his first taste of being alone inside his family.

• • •

Well, see, from The New York Times, *Janie found out the address of her real family, down in New Jersey. And one day, I'm driv-*

40

ing us to school, because we lived next
door, and I had my own Jeep, and Janie
says, "Let's cut school."

And I'm thinking of reasons that I would cut
school, and things I would do with Janie if
we were alone all day long, and Janie
says, "Let's drive to New Jersey and find
them."

So we drove to New Jersey.

And we found them.

Remember I told you about Janie's hair? Serious hair. As much hair as any two or three
regular people. Auburn-copper hair that she
wore long. Once the physics teacher de-
fined chaos as Janie's hair. And there, on
the right street, across from the right house,
a school bus stops. And kids with the very
same red hair get off. The hair—and presumably, therefore, the genes—are a perfect match. Janie really is the sister.

I'm hanging on to the steering wheel with
white knuckles, I'm so surprised. I hadn't
believed it till then. I'm almost sick. Because I like Janie's parents as much as I
like my own. How could they steal Janie
and still be nice? There couldn't be a nice
answer to that. There could only be a terrible answer. And Janie, my poor Janie, is
practically on the floor of the Jeep, hiding
from them, so they can't see her hair and
know who she has to be, whispering,
"Drive on, keep driving, get out of here,
Reeve."

So we got out of there. We didn't tell. We didn't

41

tell our families in Connecticut, or the authorities, or the family in New Jersey. But we knew. We knew it was true. Janie Johnson had been kidnapped. So there was the same question. Always the same question. Now what?

•   •   •

Mrs. Spring watched her family heading for bed. Her husband went down the hall to shut off the computer. Her big, hulking thirteen-year-old, Brendan, took the stairs two at a time. Already his immense sneakers had left black scuff marks on the freshly painted risers. Her small, thin thirteen-year-old, Brian, followed slowly, dragging.

She had to be a better mother and not go out at these ridiculous hours on a school night; this was way too late for Brian.

Upstairs, doors closed, shoes dropped, faucets ran. She loved having everybody upstairs and safe.

She looked happily around her living room.

New furniture would arrive tomorrow. She was excited. All this space in which to put lovely, comfy furniture. Big, fat easy chairs to flop on and curl up on with a book. Big, roomy couches to nap on or watch television on. A dining table to fit everybody comfortably, including aunts, uncles and neighbors.

Everybody except Jennie.

Jennie, who had happily gone back to being Janie.

Every time Mrs. Spring got too busy to remember, there it was again, creeping like a vine, twisting itself around the good things and strangling them.

The loss of Jennie.

In some terrible way, deep and black as an abandoned coal mine, Mrs. Spring was still waiting.

Waiting for Jennie to come home.

CHAPTER
FOUR

It was Lipstick Day. You had to do something to kick off a dud month like November.

Everybody—boys and girls—slathered on bright red or Halloween orange or hot-pink lipstick. The goal was to acquire as many lip prints on your face as possible.

Janie was fully printed, her face covered with neatly outlined lips. Some people smeared on their kisses, but Janie made them do it neatly or not at all.

Ordinary kids became barbarians getting ready for battle. They were live theater art: a stage event for face patterns.

Nobody kissed on the lips. That wasn't the point. You were writing on people.

Of course, there were the skanky kids, that you didn't even want to be in the same room with, or share a calculator with, and you were supposed to purse your lips together and plant a serious kiss on their cheek. In these situations, you fell to the floor in your death throes rather than kiss them.

Sarah-Charlotte had some really evil lipstick colors. "My mother didn't get the color gene," explained Sarah-Charlotte, "so the house is full of disgusting purple-bruise lipsticks." During lunch,

Sarah-Charlotte passed these out to people who had come unarmed.

Janie felt light.

Not low-fat light; not a substitute. Janie's light was whipped cream or the scent of lilacs. Today she was the right person for her hair: She was an armload of red. I'm back, thought Janie. You do get past the bad parts. I'm here, I'm me, I know what I'm doing.

"Janie," said Van, who had shaved his head and consequently had much more lip print space than people with hair, "I covet your print."

"My print is pretty special," agreed Janie. She had always liked Van. When you were steadily dating a boy, as she was Reeve, and this was known to everybody, it freed you up to be friends with boys. You could skip the worry factor, the impress-him factor. "Where do you want your print, Van?"

"I've given skull space to ordinary lips," said Van, "but for you, Jane Elizabeth Johnson, I have reserved an entire jawbone."

There was a round of applause and whistles.

Sarah-Charlotte repainted Janie's lips a revolting magenta, so much lipstick that it felt like pancake batter. Janie held Van's head between her hands to steady it and aimed carefully for the wide part of his jaw. She planted her kiss firmly and long. Then she stepped back to admire her handiwork.

Sarah-Charlotte, who thought of details nobody else remembered until it was too late, had brought a large hand mirror, in which Van admired his jaw.

One year ago, in this cafeteria, a little girl on the back of a milk carton had stared out at Janie

Johnson. The photo had shown an ordinary toddler: hair in tight pigtails, one against each thin cheek. A dress with a narrow collar and tiny, dark polka dots. Janie had clung to that cardboard while her mind slipped and her brain turned to glass. *She remembered that dress.*

Janie had shouted Sarah-Charlotte's name, trying to tell her best friend that good had just changed to evil, but her lips had not moved. She had made no sound.

It seemed to Janie now that for months she had made no sound. But today the past was past. This was just school, full of friends and cheeks and jaws.

Janie heard herself laugh, and she recognized the laugh: pre–milk carton laughter. She could hardly wait to telephone Reeve: I'm here, I'm laughing!

After school, Sarah-Charlotte wanted to go show off their lip prints. The only real choice was the volleyball game. Janie had never cared for volleyball. She had never figured out how to serve without hurting her wrist, and although she was less afraid of a volleyball than of a baseball, still she hated a ball coming at her. She was awestruck by athletes who loved balls coming at them, who leaped forward and flung themselves into the path of the ball.

She and Sarah-Charlotte sat on bleachers in the midst of a crowd of printed cheeks.

Yearbook photographers converged on the pack. Tyler, who was in charge of candids, closed in on Janie.

Janie shook her head and turned her face away.

"Come on, look at the camera, Janie, give me a full-face shot!" Tyler leaped up the bleachers, missing innocent people's hair and glasses by microns. He took three shots with Janie's hand in the way. Janie glared at him and he snapped that, too.

"Stop it! I'm not a senior."

"We need it for the yearbook, Janie. We're going to do a milk carton page."

"What are you talking about?"

"Come on, Janie. You're famous. The face on the milk carton. We lived through you. People have scrapbooks about you. We're going to have the whole thing in the yearbook."

This terrible part of her life she wanted forgotten? And they were going to make a separate section in the yearbook?

How could she touch a yearbook ruined like that? What if people signed her yearbook and nobody wrote *I'll miss you, what great times we had, good luck!* but instead they wrote *Your kidnapping story was so exciting, I'll always remember the time network TV came to the school.*

TV, which had tried to slice her up, ruin her family, chase them down, make her parents admit that this tragedy was their fault—*this* would get a yearbook page?

Janie wanted to rip the camera out of Tyler's hands. She wanted to yank out the film, tear it into pieces with her bare hands.

So she did.

She had had only Tyler's attention. Now she had the entire gym gaping at her. Parents and teachers rushed to referee. Janie was freaked, and looked like a freak. Face coated with flaming lip prints, hands trying to kill a camera.

I've got to get out of here, thought Janie, and she started to plunge down the bleachers, to run for the girls' room, scrub the lipstick off her face, hide out. Janie had spent plenty of time hiding out: under the covers, in girls' rooms in New Jersey and Connecticut high schools, behind her hair, behind her silence.

"Don't run," said Sarah-Charlotte quietly, forcing her back down on the bleacher. "Just smile and wait. They'll go." Sarah-Charlotte handed the empty camera back to Tyler. "Beat it, Ty."

"I have to get out of here," whispered Janie, "they're staring at me."

"Stare back. *But don't you run.*"

Janie felt as exposed and unraveled as the film hanging from her hand. But Sarah-Charlotte was right. In a minute or two, people had moved on, watching the game, leaving Janie alone.

"Primitive response," explained Sarah-Charlotte, "is fight or flight. But you can't do both. You're always doing both at once, Janie. You're the one tearing yourself apart. Next time you start a fight, stay in the fight."

How come Sarah-Charlotte, who never had problems, was the one with wisdom? How come she, Janie, was the one who had not learned anything? This hardly seemed fair.

"I believe," said Sarah-Charlotte, "that last year, your response was flight, the whole flight, and nothing but the flight. And look where it got you. One nightmare after another." Sarah-Charlotte made it sound as if there were no nightmare, merely Janie's failure to sit still. "This year, choose fight," instructed Sarah-Charlotte. "That way, it ends fast."

Ends.

Reeve's older sister, Lizzie, had been a lawyer for Janie. When will it end? When will it be over? Janie had asked Lizzie. When will I be an ordinary girl with an ordinary family?

It will never be over, Lizzie said.

Oh, Reeve! thought Janie. She didn't want her girlfriend. She wanted her boyfriend. Reeve, when you're here, it is over. I don't have to choose between fight or flight.

If only the chronology of being a teenager were not so rigid. After high school came college, period, and so Reeve had gone into a college world. Period.

She closed her eyes and brought him home in her heart.

• • •

WSCK was rarely able to fill requests. Requests were for commercial radio stations. WSCK played bands that were formed and fell apart in a semester, bands that chose a new name every month, bands whose name stayed the same but whose singers came and went like traffic.

Naturally no listener could remember the names of these bands, so requests were "You know, those guys on the sixth floor of Cushing Hall? With the beards? Play their tape." How were you supposed to know from the tape whether people had beards?

"Play that band you did the other day, those guys that sang, remember them?"

Derek did not stay polite to stupid people, but Reeve continued to be nice, and struggled to figure out what they meant.

But on Tuesday and Thursday evenings, the callers called about Janie.

Every week the numbers climbed. Thirty-nine no longer seemed astronomical. "Any questions?" Reeve would say, halfway through his hour. "Call the station if you need a janie boost."

They called.

Reeve could not get over how, with the mike at his mouth, he could say out loud things he never would have said in actual conversation.

He would never have told his own parents about Janie's crying jags. He had not told his best friend a single detail of the suffering Janie had forced upon the Springs. He hadn't told Sarah-Charlotte when she tried to pump him.

It had taken no effort for Reeve to keep the secrets of his girlfriend's heart and soul. Janie wanted it private, so it was private. Reeve just sat with her while she spilled over, like a glass of water. To Reeve, Janie was clear and beautiful, like spring water, while the circumstances around her were muddy and infected.

He tended to stop listening to Janie's troubles, actually, wishing this could be happening in the summer, when she would have less clothing on and he could rub sunscreen lotion on her skin. All her skin. Skin he had not yet seen.

Then he would wake up from his reverie on the beauty and wonder of girls to find that his own personal beauty and wonder was still crying about parents. He wanted to say: They're only parents! Give it a rest! Look who's holding you up! A boy. A boy who wants you so much he cannot believe that you are still talking about parents. Or even talking. Don't you realize there's a time and a place for talk, and this isn't it?

No, Janie went on failing to realize that it was time for physical involvement, instead of mental or emotional.

Reeve's sister Lizzie, now, she loved to talk, so she picked a talking profession: law.

Lizzie's head was packed with argument. She liked silence, so that she could fill it with a lecture. She liked questions, so that she could answer them at great length. She liked not getting together with her family, because they thought they should be able to talk, and this was not correct: Only Lizzie should be able to talk. Other people should listen.

Reeve felt a real kinship with Lizzie now. Other people should listen.

Of course, the question you're phoning in with is . . . who's the bad guy here? There's gotta be a bad guy. You can't have a kidnapping without a bad guy. But Reeve, you tell me over the phone, you make Janie's real parents sound like great people, and you make Janie's kidnap parents sound like great people.
There's a problem here.
Somebody has to be the bad guy.

51

You're right.
There was a bad guy.
And her name was Hannah.

• • •

Derek took over at the mike, pushing an on-air contest. "You can go to a *real* concert, instead of the crap produced on this campus!" said Derek, trying to get the phones to ring.

Derek was jealous and hurt. Vinnie fawned over Reeve. He, Derek, got treated like reliable old equipment. Reeve just trashed his girlfriend for a few sentences and the phones went crazy.

But trash sells.

The nickname of which Derek was so proud— Derek Himself—was foolish now; in one short month, he'd become nothing but Reeve's lead-in.

Derek didn't have a girlfriend. He thought Janie sounded wonderful; beautiful; the kind of girl who deserved a *Once upon a time* beginning, complete with handsome prince. Well, Janie might have a lot of stuff, but she sure didn't have a prince.

• • •

Janie didn't have her driver's license yet. Everyone else lived for the moment of getting a license. Janie didn't want one. After all these years of being so sheltered, she found that she was willing to go on being sheltered. She liked to have her mother or father drive her. She liked the comfort of getting into a car and having her parents smile at her and knowing that they would navigate and cope with traffic and she could just sit there and dream.

Last year Reeve had driven her to school, but this year it was Sarah-Charlotte. Sarah-Charlotte had one of the world's less safe cars: a teeny Yugo with a hundred thousand miles on it, its upholstery rotted and split by the hot sun in the parking lot. Passengers spread towels on the disintegrating foam and hoped to be alive after a few miles of Sarah-Charlotte's braking technique.

Sarah-Charlotte and Janie left after the volleyball game and drove to Janie's. Sarah-Charlotte clipped a curb and jumped two lights. "I'm insane to drive anywhere with you," Janie said.

"It builds your character. Whoa, look, Janie! On your porch. It's that reporter! The one who won't let go."

Janie recognized him. The question this particular reporter liked was the responsibility question. Who had created the Hannah who grew up to be a kidnapper? What had Mr. and Mrs. Johnson done so wrong, so badly, that their not-so-little girl Hannah had stolen the Springs' little girl Jennie?

"You better come home with me," said Sarah-Charlotte.

But Janie's beautiful house, designed to be open to sun and sky, was blank. Her mother had pulled every blind and drape. "I have to go in. My mother's alone."

"Call if you need me," said her friend.

"Let's hope I won't need rescue twice in one day." Janie launched herself toward her own front door.

"Jennie Spring!" the reporter cried. "Good to see you again! It's been six months since—"

Janie neither looked at him nor spoke. She knew by now that a silent subject did not make good copy.

The door opened from the inside, and together Janie and her mother shut it against the journalist.

Janie rubbed her mother's cold hands between hers. Her mother had gotten so thin in the last year. Her fingers were bony and old. "What happened?" said Janie.

"They think their readers deserve an update."

Everybody deserves something, thought Janie. Sarah-Charlotte deserves details, Ty deserves photographs, the readers deserve a piece of my mother.

She hated them.

Janie made a pot of coffee. Coffee relaxed her mother, but it put Janie on the ceiling. She needed to be the one on the ground. So much for telling Mommy about Lipstick Day and Tyler's yearbook plans.

When Daddy got home from work and heard they'd had a reporter around, he just made it worse. Instead of brushing it aside, he actually confided, "I've been thinking about Hannah lately."

They never admitted this: that Hannah was real, a real daughter, and must be thought of.

Janie had a sudden, terrible vision of her parents with a carrying case full of Hannahs under their bed. But they couldn't take Hannah out, like a Barbie, and dress her, and fix her hair, and fix her life.

"I was on the Internet the other night," said her father. His fingertips touched his wife's, and Janie saw that her mother's ring finger had gotten so thin that she'd wrapped tape around her wedding band to keep it from falling off. "On the Internet, you're connected to a million strangers. Names without faces. Hidden people."

In the Johnson family code, this meant Hannah.

"Do you think she's out there?" whispered Janie's mother, shivering not just with fear, but also with hope. Hannah was a lost daughter. Dangerous—but still, and forevermore, a daughter.

What would we hope for, if we hoped for Hannah? thought Janie. It's too late for the good career, or the fine husband, or the healthy children.

I am their only hope, she thought. I am all that stands between them and hell.

It was Janie who insisted on dinner; Janie who assigned easy little tasks; Janie who asked casually if everybody was taking their heart medicine.

Her mother normalized. "Everybody? Well, I am, and your father is, but luckily *you* don't need heart medicine."

Oh, but I do, thought Janie. I do. And so does the world.

•   •   •

"Hi, you've reached WSCK!" said Reeve into the telephone. "We're Here, We're Yours, We're Sick! How can I help you?"

"Hi, Reeve. Are you going to do a janie tonight?" The caller had recognized Reeve's voice.

Awesome! thought Reeve. For the next call, he did a little test. "Hi, you've reached WSCK! We're

Here, We're Yours, We're Sick! This is Burt Smith, how can I help you?"

"Hi, Reeve. Burt Smith is a dumb name, don't use it. Reeve is much sexier. Listen, I just have one question. I don't understand how her kidnap parents are still the good guys."

The phone was becoming nearly as much fun as the mike.

He felt like recording these calls, proof that he meant something in this world.

Call-ins were recorded only if the deejay intended to play them on the air, and only Derek ever did that. Derek loved stupid people. Stupid people would telephone the college radio station expecting answers to college questions. "Do exams really begin Tuesday morning?"

Derek loved these. "Omigod!" he would shriek. "Exams are over! You weren't there? Oh, no, your semester means nothing now. How are you going to tell your parents you just threw away twelve thousand dollars?"

Therefore Derek tended to tape callers, in case there was a humiliating exchange he could play later. Everybody else just kept the log so that they could prove they had listeners. Reeve entered another janie.

What a difference a capital letter made. A *janie* was airtime. Drama. No person involved.

Reeve listened to Derek Himself's spinning intro, the elongated vowels—"what yooooouuuu've been waiting for!"—and the exclamation points in Derek's voice.

For me, he thought. For my voice. My story.

56

Derek slid out of the way, and Reeve took over. He fondled the fat sides of the mike.

That microphone gave him the most amazing freedom. Reeve could say anything.

And did.

Hannah.

She was pretty in a limp sort of way.

Like a used rag doll. Nobody is ever best friends with that kind. They're on the fringes. Doomed.

Hannah joined a cult, dropped out of regular life, probably thought she was one of the good guys, because her cult said that God was on their side.

Years after she left her nice home and her nice parents, Hannah kidnapped a little girl named Jennie Spring.

Why? Nobody knows. Maybe she just wanted company. A smiling face in the passenger seat. Somebody to have ice cream with. Maybe it sort of happened by itself and she didn't know what to do afterward. Or maybe she wanted that poor family to suffer. To worry, year after year: Is our little girl in pain? Is she cold? Is she scared? Is she bleeding? Is she alive?

Hannah took that little girl home to her own mom and dad, and she said, This is my baby. Your grandchild. You'll be better parents than I am, so bye! Enjoy her! And Hannah left.

She went back to her cult. Maybe. Nobody knows. Anyway, she disappeared forever, leaving only one instruction. "Enjoy her." And they did. Oh, how they enjoyed her! Their little girl—they thought her name was Janie, not Jennie—was the light of their lives. When they were parents to Hannah, they must have made some really, really big mistake, though they never figured out what the mistake was, or when they made it. But you've got to admit, good parents don't have daughters who join cults and abandon their babies. But now they could get it right. This time around, they'd be perfect parents. And Janie: It was her job to be the perfect daughter.

•　•　•

Janie took out her Barbies.

She no longer had the large accessories: cars, beauty parlor, furniture, condo—these were long gone to fund-raiser tag sales.

She still had the clothing.

She sat on her bed and sorted wardrobes by career. Barbies liked to be onstage, so there were lots of choices: singer, ballerina or model. Barbies liked the professions, so they could be doctor, astronaut or soldier. And they loved sports, so they were always ready to go horseback riding, or teach swimming, or just get a tan.

The Barbies had had more careers in that suitcase than Janie had ever daydreamed of for herself.

In fact, trapped in yearbook visions, forced to think of graduation and college, Janie realized that she had never had any plans except to stay sane and keep the number of parents in her life as low as possible.

And marriage.

She wanted to be married the way both her Johnson and her Spring parents were married: for better or for worse, so that when the worst came, you held on to each other, until better returned.

Just because Reeve hasn't checked his e-mail, hasn't called, hasn't written, doesn't mean the world is over, she told herself.

Two years.

Two *years* before she could join Reeve at college.

•   •   •

Once again Reeve had been at WSCK so many hours that the cafeteria was closed by the time he remembered dinner. He was forced to eat from a row of vending machines that lined the student center.

"Hey, aren't you the guy on Sick?" said a girl getting Fritos.

Reeve grinned and nodded. He loved being noticed.

"I'm Kerry." She offered him some of her Fritos. "You do the janie thing! I haven't missed a single janie," said Kerry, like a collector.

What a trip! Back home, recognition and admiration had gone to his older brother and sisters. No wonder they enjoyed life so much.

"I liked that part where Janie had such bad nightmares she had to barricade herself in with pillows to keep the demons from attacking her spine or her toes while she slept," said Kerry. "I had to do that when I was little."

Reeve felt a funny dryness in his mouth, as if he had seen a bear on the path. I told about that? Her parents don't know about that. Now Boston knows.

"My boyfriend Matthew is in love with Janie. He says he'd know her the minute he saw her, with that red hair swirled around her head."

It had not occurred to Reeve that he had described Janie so well that strangers could recognize her. He wanted an audience, but at the same time, he didn't want the audience to be real.

It doesn't matter, Reeve said to himself. Janie'll never hear my broadcasts. Nobody outside of Hills College listens to WSCK. I bet there are fifty stations around Boston and everybody is listening to them.

Statistics of probability always made Reeve feel better.

He walked down the street to his dorm. Hills College had no grass, no quadrangles; it simply filled several Boston blocks. Reeve had not explored Boston the way the other freshmen had. They went shopping on Newbury Street, or skated on Rollerblades down Commonwealth, or headed out Mass Av to Cambridge. He knew enough not to pronounce *Av Avenue,* but he had not actually taken the road himself. WSCK had absorbed him.

60

He picked his way around torn-up pavement and huge yellow equipment in front of his dorm. You couldn't call it a construction site; nobody ever seemed to work here. It was more like a parking lot for bulldozers.

He skipped the dorm elevator and took four flights of stairs two steps at a time. Speed made Reeve feel better, too.

Three boys were getting off the elevator near his room. Nobody Reeve knew. Computer geeks. You were supposed to refer to your fellow students as men and women, but sometimes the words didn't fit. These were boys.

"Hi," said one boy timidly. "We're Visionary Assassins."

"*You* are?" said Reeve. This trio would have trouble looking both ways before they crossed a street, never mind being assassins.

"We're here to thank you." They were visibly delighted to meet him. He was Somebody. "You play us whenever you're on. We're your signature. Everybody's talking about the janies now, and they think of us at the same time. We just got our first paid gig because of you."

His radio show worked. It meant something!

"Can you announce on the next janie that we're going to be playing Saturday at Peaches n Crude?" they said anxiously. "We'd love it if you'd come, Reeve."

Reeve did not want them to see how happy he was. Famous people were cool. So he didn't leap into the air and smash through the ceiling panels with his fist. He said, "I might." He gave a casual good-night salute and opened his door.

Cordell now had a steady girlfriend, and he had given Pammy a key to their room. Reeve was just as apt to find Pammy living there as Cordell. He was still getting used to girls in various stages of undress sharing his actual bedroom. College was definitely different from home.

Pammy draped herself around Reeve, who peeled her off like a sweater and set her aside.

"We were just talking about you," said Pammy. "What was in the box in the attic? You never went back to that."

How strange to be quoted.

"Come on, Reevey, tell."

"If you call me Reevey," said Reeve, "I'm going to put a hand grenade in your cereal."

"But what *was* in the box?" asked Cordell. "I'm your roomie. You have to tell me. College rule."

Reeve had a vision of his audience. The unwashed Cordells and the worthless Pammys. The dry, unpleasant taste filled his mouth.

"It would be easier to keep track of the story if you'd use last names," said Cordell.

Last names Reeve omitted because that way it wasn't the Johnsons and the Springs; it was generic; it could be any kidnap family in this situation.

Not that there was any other family in this situation.

Reeve busied himself with their shared computer. Maybe he had mail. He never went past the dorm letter boxes without checking for a written letter, but he preferred e-mail. Written letters were exhausting. They required written answers. Reeve hated handwriting. Steering that little stick with the ink at the bottom of it was a chore he had never conquered. When he had to handwrite, the words got cramped into the upper corners of the page, and his fingers hurt, and his brain went dead.

At the computer, there was no long, blank page like an accusation from a teacher that he hadn't finished the assignment.

Another cool thing about e-mail was that for some reason spelling didn't matter, and if you were a terrible typist, that didn't matter either; you didn't have to do it over. The first time was always good enough.

If I go into radio, thought Reeve, I can skip handwriting. My life will be wired.

YOU HAVE MAIL, said the cute little blinking postman icon.

Reeve smiled idiotically, the way people do when someone writes to them, personally. The letter was from Janie.

> Reeve, I've had the worst day. Of course I did something stupid and made it worse. Reeve, I need you. Can I come up and visit you? Mommy and Daddy would never let me stay overnight, but I could stay all day. I could go to class with you, I wouldn't get in your way. I'd take the train that arrives in Boston at 9:22 a.m. How's Friday? Loooooooovvvvvvve Janie

CHAPTER
FIVE

Reeve's hair prickled. He hated that feeling, as if his hair had come alive, or he had lice. Janie here? On campus? It was the hair that would give it away, just as that hair had been proof from the beginning. He remembered the spread of that coppery-red mass; the right he had, as boyfriend, to play with it, and kiss the face hidden beneath it.

Reeve imagined himself and Janie bumping into Vinnie. Or Derek Himself. Pammy or Cordell. Kerry's boyfriend Matthew. They'd know in a heartbeat who she had to be.

Reeve had known he shouldn't be doing this, but it was such fun that he had pretended he didn't know.

He had been doing the janies for a month now. They were the major part of his life. Reeve so routinely cut classes that he hardly thought of himself as having any.

How was he to handle a college visit? He was hardly even a college student.

If I don't take her to the student center, he thought, and I don't take her to my dorm, which I'll say is all grungy disgusting guys, which is true, and I tell her I've got to get off campus, being cooped up here is making me insane, and think how much there is to see and do in Boston . . . we could go straight from the train to Quincy Market, Janie loves shopping. Take her to some elegant restaurant like Legal Seafoods. Dinner at that kind of restaurant takes hours, no time to visit the campus, got to rush to Back Bay Station.

He clicked his mail closed. It vanished in a screen sort of way, sucking itself backward into the hardware.

• • •

Janie lay on her bed, flipping through TV stations with her remote. Talk show after talk show. Why did the rest of world love witnesses? How could they hop onto TV and blurt out their entire lives without a twitch? To ten million witnesses?

The phone rang.

"Hello," she said. She wanted Reeve the way she wanted oxygen. She pressed Mute on her remote. The talk show hostess struck silent, dramatic poses and thrust the mike into the faces of eager audience members. You could tell the audience was after blood.

"Hey, Janie," said Reeve. "What made the day so awful? Tell me about it."

"Oh, Reeve! I'm so glad you called. I was afraid you wouldn't check your e-mail. Sarah-Charlotte is smarter than I am, is what happened." If only she could picture him now—where he was, how the room was shaped, what he sat on, the color of the phone, what he was wearing.

She missed all of him, all ways. Talk for hours, she thought, tell me everything, blot away today.

"This is about Sarah-Charlotte's IQ? Who cares?" said Reeve.

"No, it's about fight or flight. Sarah-Charlotte knew all along and I still haven't figured it out."

"Talking to you always starts in the middle," said Reeve.

"I know, and the best thing about you is, you always catch up." Janie told him about Lipstick Day, which he loved.

"That's great! We didn't do that when I was in school. Whose idea was that?" said Reeve.

"Sarah-Charlotte's. You know her. People obey her. So even with this weird idea that I didn't think a single person would participate in, five hundred people did."

"I wish I'd seen you. Anybody take photographs?"

"Oh, Reeve! That's the point! I tried to kill the kid who tried to take my picture!" She told him about the scene in the gym.

The silent TV disrupted her thoughts, so she clicked it off, getting rid of the confessing guest and the avid audience. Even without sound, it was clear that a second guest was hearing something he hadn't known; hadn't wanted to know; was hearing for the first time ever in front of the world.

How could people cut out their own hearts—or the heart of a person they used to love? And then hand it around, a little joke between commercials?

"Reeve, I'm just material to them. I'm not a person. I'm a page in a yearbook."

He didn't answer for a moment. Then, strained, he said, "That's awful, Janie."

She loved the anxiety in his voice. "Oh, Reeve, I want to talk, I want to come up and visit you."

"That would be great. I'd love to see you. But I don't know where you'd stay. My roommate is too disgusting for you even to meet. And it's so crowded; every double room's a triple this year. I don't know any girls I could ask to take a guest."

"But I want to get away, Reeve, to where it's safe and nobody knows me."

He laughed oddly. She did not know what to make of it. "If you had been at school, Reeve, it would have been okay. I would have put a lip print on your cheek."

"I would have reserved my cheeks for your prints exclusively."

"Send me those kisses over the phone," she ordered.

He sent kisses over the phone.

"Send me a tape of your show," she said.

"I don't do anything. I'm the new kid. Besides, college radio plays pretty rough stuff. Your parents would pass out if they heard the lyrics I've memorized."

"Sing me some," said Janie.

"When I get home," he promised.

•   •   •

Reeve lay on his back in the lower bunk and stared up at the blue-striped bottom of Cordell's mattress. There was no privacy in a college dorm. He had to think things through in the middle of a room full of people he detested.

If Janie was hurt by a page in the yearbook . . .

if she had grabbed the guy's camera, and nearly smashed it on the gym floor, all but hit him in the face with it . . .

She shouldn't be so sensitive, he told himself. She's not in step with the decade. This is routine. Everybody airs their emotions in public.

He imagined Janie lying here beside him, snuggled in on the wall side of the bunk. He had ended any chance of bringing Janie into his college life.

So don't do it again, he told himself, don't stay at the radio station, don't do any more janies.

Very early that morning, long before it was light, Reeve got up, dressed warmly, and left the dorm for a different kind of station.

•   •   •

The day after Lipstick Day had the first truly winter-is-coming weather of the school year. Janie wore layers. Winter clothes felt safer than summer clothes. She put on a hunter-green river driver shirt and tucked it into a darker green corduroy skirt. She yanked on trail walkers, padded for hiking, and laced the boots tightly. She tied a scarf around her neck and shrugged into an extra-large tweed blazer. For earrings she picked out heavy dangling silver moons, crescents to swing beneath her red hair. Janie loved earrings and had a huge collection, but never fixed her hair so that her ears showed. She kept meaning to analyze this but had never gotten around to it.

After breakfast she kissed her parents good-bye. "What are you guys grinning about?" she said suspiciously.

They pointed outside. It looked pretty ordinary

to Janie. Nothing out there but their driveway, pocked with ice-rimmed puddles, and the Shieldses' driveway and Reeve's Jeep waiting for her—

"Reeve!" she shrieked.

She whirled around and hugged her parents. "Did you know he was coming?"

"His mother called before you were up. He was in the mood to see you and he caught the dawn train out of Boston," said her father. He was smiling in the way of parents whose children are happy before their eyes.

"Ooooh!" said Janie. "How romantic!"

"Have a great day," said her mother.

"I will! There is no doubt of that! None!" Janie spun out of the house. How wonderful the Jeep looked, idling away, Reeve grinning at her from the driver's seat. He leaned over to open the passenger door with his right hand, but she ignored that, raced around the car and ripped open his door.

When they finished hugging, he looked her up and down. "You going fishing maybe? Hiking the Appalachian Trail?"

"At least I look interesting. You look exactly the same as you did last year. Rugby shirt, khakis, loafers, no socks."

"It's the boy-next-door look."

"I thought once you went to college you'd act out. Wear gang clothes, or get tattoos."

Reeve gave her a look. "You want tattoos? I'll get tattoos. Where do you want your initials?"

"Ugh! No! Don't even think about it. I hate tattoos. I just thought that eighteen-year-old boys at college went wild."

Reeve shook his head. "No, that's girls."

"Oh. Do you think I'll go wild when I get out of town?"

Reeve laughed. He had been asking her to go wild for two years. "There's always hope."

She wanted to sit in his lap for the drive to school. That long, thin face with that big, wide grin, so that when he laughed, there was nothing on his face but laugh. He'd gotten a buzz last year, but never trimmed it, so now the hair was in desperate need of cutting, but at the same time perfect, as if he were a windblown model. Reeve drove with his left hand and slipped his right hand under her hair, at the back of her neck, and his big made-for-footballs hand lay warm and wonderful against her pulse.

Reeve discovered the earrings. He grinned, tucked her hair back and untangled the crescent moons from her curls.

"Oh, Reeve, forget school, let's skip," she said. "The way we did that New Jersey day."

"No, I'm coming in with you. I'm going to attend classes with you."

"You're kidding."

"I think they'll let me. But actually, I'm not going to ask. I've learned one entire thing at college. Don't ask. Just do it." He grinned again. Janie would take bets. No teacher at her high school was going to turn down a guy with that grin.

Reeve proceeded to disrupt Janie's English class by gluing his eyes on her and never moving, never blinking. She felt his eyes right through her hair. She twitched and shifted, wrapped her hair in a ponytail and let it go, rested her chin in her hands, and then tilted sideways to see if he was still staring.

He was.

Every girl was envious, and every boy wondered how Reeve had acquired the composure to demonstrate so vividly how he felt about a girl.

In the halls Reeve wound his fingers through her hair, and they walked in step, half leaning on each other.

Tyler, camera bouncing on his chest, saw them coming. He pantomimed a photograph, but Reeve shook his head.

I was going to say yes! thought Janie. When people stare at me because I'm a milk carton freak, I could kill them. But stares because we make a cute couple—I love it. "I have gym now, Reeve," she said regretfully. "It's really unlikely that they're going to let you in the girls' locker room."

"It's okay. I have stuff to do," he said breezily. "People to blackmail, places to rob."

She didn't see him again till lunch, when he scooped her up and said they were going to Mickey D's. The school had just started letting kids go off campus for lunch. You had to have parental permission, and Janie, of course, had no such thing.

She and Reeve sauntered out of the building, following his rule of Don't ask, just do it, and nobody in authority noticed, and everybody in the student body did.

She'd be delighted to have a yearbook page for the romance of Reeve Shields and Janie Johnson.

He opened the Jeep door for her. They loved doing things for each other. When she was seated, he tucked her skirt in so that it wouldn't get caught in

71

the door, and it felt like being tucked in at night. He started the engine and revved it a few times. "That's my heart," he told her, and they laughed.

"What did you do during my last two classes, Reeve?"

"Found the yearbook adviser. Told her she can't allow a milk carton page. She promised. It's not gonna happen."

Last year Janie would have wept all over him. This year she burst into laughter. "Oh, Reeve, you make everything so simple! I can't stand it that you're a million miles away."

"It's not even two hundred miles."

"Light-years, then."

They skipped lunch.

They found the far rear of McDonald's parking lot instead, and Reeve said, "You are wearing very heavy-duty clothes, Janie."

"We trail walkers have to fend off attacking mosquitoes and grizzly bears."

"Just don't fend *me* off," said Reeve.

CHAPTER
SIX

"I want to drive up to Boston, Mom," said Jodie.

Mom, Brian and Jodie were at Home Depot, tracking down window blinds and kitchen-cabinet knobs. Brendan's team had practice, of course; Brian had hardly seen his twin for days.

"There are six colleges I want to look at in Boston," said Brian's sister. "Friday we have a teachers' workshop, so there's no school; I can drive up to Boston Thursday after school, have Friday and Saturday to tour campuses and do interviews, and then drive back Sunday."

"By yourself?" said Mom doubtfully. Not as if she were going to lash out and shriek *NO, NO, NEVER!* but as if Jodie were brave to take on traffic and navigation all the way to Boston. "Maybe if you had company it would be okay."

Jodie nodded. "I'd like company, but Caitlin and Nicole are going south, they're looking in Virginia for colleges." A year ago, Brian thought, Jodie would not have dared mention going to a city at all, never mind alone.

Their mother said, "But your father and I want to go along when you visit campuses, Jo. And that weekend we'll be so busy. Brendan has *two* games." Their parents had never missed a game, performance or concert in which one of their children had participated.

"Mom, I'm running out of time!" said Jodie. "I have to decide where I'm applying in only a few months."

Brian was not eager to see Brendan triumph twice in one weekend, and Boston sounded great, plus he was mildly fond of his sister, so he said, "I'll go with you, Jodie. I can read the maps and hand you change for the tolls."

"That's wonderful!" Jodie hugged him right there in the store. Brian shrank out from under her grasp and took refuge on the far side of the cart.

"But Brian," said his mother, "Brendan has a big game on Friday afternoon, and another one on Saturday. He's your twin," she added, as if Brian, of all people, might have forgotten this.

"Mom, I've seen Brendan play. I'll see him the rest of my life. But I haven't been to Boston with Jodie." Boston is history, he thought. Ben Franklin, John Adams, John Hancock, Paul Revere. Maybe I'll go to college in Boston, too, and study history.

He had never had a long view of his life. His life was in short takes: a practice, a game, a shower, a brother. Now he could see it, his own personal calendar years spread like computer printouts.

One day last week, when Bren had practice and Brian didn't, Brian had gone to the town library and wandered through the adult American history section. He had never entered the adult division of the library before. He'd felt like a trespasser. The collection was immense. He didn't know where to begin. How did you figure out which of those thousands of books you wanted to read?

He settled for reading the spines, just exploring titles. The books were arranged like geography, starting with European explorers crossing the Atlantic, moving into settlers of New England, and advancing toward the Ohio River, the Great Lakes, and the Mississippi.

He came home after two hours in which nobody had known where he was. And when he got home, nobody asked. It was a first in Brian's thirteen years.

He wanted to thank his parents. He wanted to shout *Yes! It's about time!* but he said nothing, because maybe they hadn't realized the freedom they had allowed, and maybe they wouldn't allow it again.

He resolved that next time, he would actually sit in one of the cozy armchairs in the adult section and read the first paragraphs of some of those books, and even take one home.

"We could stop off at the Johnsons'," said Jodie eagerly, "and see Janie."

Any idea that they had a new, easy, upbeat life vanished.

Their mother's face sagged and she looked blindly at her shopping list, swallowing hard as she checked off an item they hadn't yet bought.

Brian was becoming the person he should have been, but his mother could never be the person she should have been.

The damage had been too long, and too terrible.

Oh, Hannah, he thought. What you did to us.

• • •

Derek Himself loved to talk about fame. "Did you see me on *20/20* last night?" Derek liked to ask. "I'm America's newest shock jock, syndicated in a hundred and seventy-two stations. They had to interview me, or their ratings would tumble."

Reeve, listening, thought: I'm the one here who might actually accomplish those things. And now I have to back off.

He'd been so surprised by his visit home. Nothing had changed. His life was so different that he had somehow expected everybody else's life to be different, too. The same pots were stacked on the same stove. The same pile of bills waited for attention on the same counter. He had forgotten high school, too, but there it sat: same halls, teachers, lights, sounds, smell.

And Janie.

He'd forgotten the silk of her hair.

Forgotten what it was like to be the physical center of someone's universe.

Forgotten, here among other young men pushing and shoving for ratings, what it was like just to be loved.

He'd felt so great, saving her from the yearbook assault.

That evening Reeve and Janie sprawled on the sofa in his parents' living room, Janie half in his lap, leaning back against his chest, holding his arms locked around her, while he rested his chin on her head. If he relaxed his hug, she'd pull his arms tight again, for that combination of love and safety that she required of him.

76

She filled him in on the reporter who had tried to barge into her house on Lipstick Day. It was good that she could not see Reeve's face. He was doing exactly what Tyler and the reporter had tried to do, except they had failed, and Reeve hadn't.

Reeve's answers, therefore, required detour after detour. It was like the streets of Boston: one pit after another. Every sentence led to WSCK, and he couldn't even mention it, let alone brag. How he wanted to tell her: Janie, I'm the *best*, I'm a fad, people tune in just for *me*.

He wanted Janie to light up, the way she did, all the way to her fingertips, laughing her wonderful laugh, and kissing him before she got her laugh done.

On the train returning to Boston, it was an easy decision: back off, skip radio.

But here in the studio . . .

Derek had put on the Fog, had a tape by Slow Burn ready to play back to back. Plenty of time for Vinnie, Cal, Derek and Reeve to talk. Talking was what they liked best. There were no strong, silent types in radio.

Back off didn't mean quit. Back off meant still here, but not as deejay. Or as deejay, but not doing janies.

If I'm here, listening to Derek Himself, can I stand it? I'd rip the mike out of his hands and do a janie anyway. I'm not gonna back off. So I have to quit. Cold. The way people who have quit smoking have to throw away their cigarettes.

Not come down here again.

Not hang out with these guys.

Find a new set of friends.

"Vinnie," he said, and he found it surprisingly hard to get enough air beneath his sentence, as if this were his first time on the radio all over again, "I'm going to quit."

"No, you're not. You love this."

"I do love it. But Janie is a real person. This would upset her. So I'm quitting."

Vinnie was amused. "You won't quit. You love the sound of your voice. You love the numbers, how you're up every week. You're an addict."

I am not. I am in control and I've made a decision. I won't do another janie.

The music was fading out. Derek Himself talked over the last chords. Reeve hated that, when they cut out the final lyrics in order to have more time for their own voices. He wasn't going to be that kind of deejay.

Derek surprised Reeve by giving him a janie cue, swinging the adjustable arm of the mike into Reeve's face.

The air was empty and waiting.

I won't say a janie, he ordered himself.

He didn't.

He swung the mike back to Derek and walked out of the broadcast room.

There. For Janie's sake, he'd quit.

He was proud of himself. He felt tall and strong and good for people. Maybe he'd run for President.

•　　•　　•

In the big Dodge coming back from Home Depot, Jodie needed to be private, so she let Brian have the front seat with Mom and she sat way in the back, slumped down, her face hidden by the middle seats.

Unbelievable. Her mother was going to allow it! Jodie would be permitted choice, and independence, and risk.

Risk.

It had never been allowed in the Spring family since Jennie had vanished.

Stephen, out there in Colorado, told them nothing when they were on the phone with him. *Nothing.* Was he being dull and good, going to class, getting eight hours of sleep, being friends with suitable people?

Or was he taking risks? Hitchhiking? Skydiving?

Jodie hoped he was taking risks.

Jodie, like the rest of the family, had hair that glinted red and gold. But unlike Janie, whose chaotic curls were airborne in the humidity of New England, Jodie's was thin and straight. She wore it in a soccer cut.

If she went to college in Boston, she'd probably dye it blue. Shave some off. Have earrings in her scalp. Scare normal people by sitting down next to them. Or maybe not. Maybe she'd wear long black skirts and vests with a zillion glitter beads. Or she might rip down the city streets on her Rollerblades, with her leather jacket and her gang bandanna.

What do I want from life, thought Jodie, now that I have choices?

Well, I don't want a family. That's more risk than I'm willing to touch. I don't have daydreams

79

with little kids in them. I don't want babies I could lose.

I'm going to have money, and answering machines, and a staff to order around, and jets, and travel, and great clothes. After my shaved-skull-and-earrings stage, that is.

And Jodie was happy, thinking: It's over.

• • •

It was cold out, the kind of cold Reeve liked. He was in shirtsleeves, but the cold felt good. He loved his bare arms in winter.

Reeve often rehearsed the janies in the dark. In front of people, he couldn't even rehearse inside his head. Alone in the dark, he could move his lips, or even whisper, getting the flow.

I have to stop that, too, he thought. I'm doing this for Janie and I don't even get to tell her what a great guy I am. No fair making sacrifices when the sacrificed-for doesn't know.

His physics professor walked by.

The science building was next door to the administration building, but still, this late—Reeve was a little surprised. "Hi, Dr. Brookner."

"Reeve," said the professor with pleasure.

Considering there were five hundred students in the lecture, the labs were run by assistants, and tests were corrected by grad students, it was remarkable that Dr. Brookner knew who Reeve was. "Doing a janie tonight?" asked the professor. "My wife and I have been fascinated by those."

Adult listeners? Professors? Reeve was stunned and pleased. "It doesn't seem like your kind of station," said Reeve.

"We put up with so-called music from losers like Visionary Assassins so that we can hear the janies. I admit I'm confused. I hope one of these days you'll clarify how the whole thing happened. My wife has a chart by the radio so we can keep track of the tidbits you dole out."

So his master plan was working. The delivery of overlapping stories, out of order, had hooked the audience.

I'll do just one more, he thought. I owe it to my audience to let them understand how the kidnapping happened. Then I'll quit.

The professor patted his shoulder. "Now if you'd work as hard at physics as you do at radio . . . ," he said, letting his voice drift off in a friendly fashion.

Reeve was aware of the cold again. It felt wonderful. It cleansed his worries. It seemed enough that he had considered quitting.

CHAPTER
SEVEN

Jodie had been counting days, hours and minutes till her first college search weekend. She could hardly wait to get into the car, get out on that interstate, and cross those state lines. O Freedom!

She drove fast and silently, dreaming of college.

The Johnsons lived about two-thirds of the way to Boston. Jodie and Brian arrived around five.

Much to Jodie's disgust, Janie's friend Sarah-Charlotte was there. Jodie considered Sarah-Charlotte the most pretentious name she had ever come across, and Sarah-Charlotte the most pretentious person. Sarah-Charlotte couldn't stand it if you abbreviated her name, so of course Jodie always wanted to call her Char.

Brian sat in the deep-blue living room and talked about libraries with Mrs. Johnson, who worked in the high school library, while Janie, Sarah-Charlotte and Jodie went upstairs to Janie's room.

"You did the room over!" exclaimed Jodie. Last time she had been here, the room had been pastel, romantic and soft. Now it was icily white. It was urban, out of a slick magazine, as if some cold, successful woman lived here with two possessions and an empty refrigerator.

You could have been in the mood to decorate a room at our house, Janie, thought Jodie resentfully. You could have let *my* mom pick out—

Jodie calmed herself. She had been mad at her sister long enough. She had not come here to pick a fight, although that had appeal and was one of Jodie's better skills.

Jodie circled the bed which looked clean and starched enough to do surgery on. There on the floor was an array of dolls. "Barbie and Ken?" she said incredulously. "Janie, they sure don't match this room."

"Come on," said Sarah-Charlotte, "Barbie has outfits to match everything."

"I wouldn't know. I never went through a doll stage." Jodie made a decision. "Sarah-Charlotte, I'm going to be incredibly rude and ask if you could visit another time, because I have only tonight to be alone with my sister." Jodie held her breath.

But to her credit, Sarah-Charlotte said she should have realized that, and she'd see Janie in school tomorrow. She ran lightly down the stairs.

In the snowiness of the white room, the sisters looked at each other edgily. They heard Brian call good-bye to Sarah-Charlotte, heard Brian and Janie's parents laugh together.

Janie flushed. "You guys are so nice when you come up here. You're polite to my parents and you joke with my dad and compliment my mother on her color schemes. I never did any of that when I visited you."

"You could start," said Jodie. She had not meant to touch the serious stuff, and here it was— too soon, too much of it. "You could start by calling

83

our parents Mom and Dad. They've stopped calling you Jennie. They've given you back completely. We don't even refer to Jennie Spring. We call you Janie Johnson. They need a present from you, Janie."

Janie felt ill and nervy. It was all this talk of futures. She didn't like to look out there the way other kids did. Janie looked ahead for a week or a month at most. Anything else was scary. "Jodie, I still have to put the words *New Jersey* first. New Jersey Mom. New Jersey Dad."

"I'm not demanding," said Jodie. She picked up a Barbie and stared at the doll as if she had never come across such an oddity. "It would just be a nice gift."

A gift, thought Janie. Barbies you wrapped for children at Christmas were just presents. But her New Jersey parents needed a gift.

Janie felt light again, her thoughts spinning off, leaving her less to work with. "The visits to New Jersey," she said finally, "were easier with Reeve."

"I know. I'm so jealous. There are no Reeves in my entire high school. Or if they're there, they're keeping a low profile."

"Saving themselves for college," agreed Janie.

I know so little about her! thought Jodie. It's Sarah-Charlotte who shared her Barbies and sleepovers. I don't want a fight. So here's a safe topic, take it. "Speaking of college," she said, "how does Reeve like it?"

"He loves it. He's not studying. His parents don't know that yet. If he flunks out in his first semester they're going to kill him."

"Reeve dead wouldn't be half so fun," said Jodie.

"Every time he calls, I nag him to study."

"I hear that boys don't like to be nagged."

"Me too, but it's irresistible. You always want to take the boy and mold him into something better."

"Name one thing that could be better about Reeve. I not only don't have a perfect boyfriend, I don't have a boyfriend," said Jodie gloomily. "Yours adores you and calls you up and e-mails you and faxes you and beeps you."

Janie giggled. "He did the first week. And a little bit the second week. But he's got a hobby now and he doesn't think of me as often. My father says it's healthier that way."

Both girls rolled their eyes at the foolishness of fathers.

"He's on a radio show," said Janie.

"No way! Tell me about it."

"College station. Volunteer stuff. He says he's just a gofer but he's learning to be a deejay."

"And he has such a great voice. All deep and sensuous. Does he just introduce the songs or does he get to talk?"

"I think he says things like the temperature outside."

"I bet it sounds wonderful when he says it. Romantic, appealing forty-four degrees. Still, if I were in Boston," said Jodie, "I'm not sure I'd listen to a college station. Aren't there better choices?" Oops! she thought, as Janie stiffened.

No. Clearly there were no better choices than Reeve in Boston. Probably in the world.

Jodie wanted to laugh at Janie and say something really barbed-wire, but they weren't sisters enough to tease over important things. It's too late, thought Jodie.

The beautiful calendar of high school graduation and college was suddenly agony. They would never be sisters under the same roof now. They might one day be friends—but sisters? Bickering, sharing, shopping, just *knowing* each other? It was too late.

"Boston sounds so wonderful," Jodie said, trying not to let her voice break. "Equal parts city and suburb. Half college campus and half insurance-company towers. There has to be so much going on, and I'm tired of a small town, aren't you? I want the big city—sidewalks, and a hundred thousand people my own age, and a dorm with all those different kinds of people, so I can learn how to get along."

"If you got along with me," said Janie, "I'd say you have it licked already."

Jodie was touched by this remark. She wanted to hug her sister and say It's all right, but it wasn't yet all right, and they were stuck in this shiny white room with furniture in between them.

"What are you going to study in college?" said Janie.

"International banking. Doesn't that sound fabulous? Wall Street and Tokyo and Zurich and London. Plus my Japanese is great after three years of studying. Might as well use it."

"Numbers," pointed out Janie, who detested math.

"I love numbers," said Jodie. "I love that word *crunch*. I can crunch any numbers on any screen. Plus, I want to be famous for something other than having a kidnapped sister." All her resolve couldn't

86

keep the next sentence from spilling out. "I still hate you for that, you know."

Judging by the flush that covered her face, Janie knew.

• • •

"Oh, good," said Jodie at the dinner table, "I love Boston Chicken." Actually she was sick of it, but right now she was setting an example for Janie. This is how you behave to your parents. Or ex-parents, or semiparents, or whatever the Springs were to Janie.

Mrs. Johnson said, "I was going to cook a meal, I've been meaning to cook a meal for weeks now, I've even looked in the direction of my cookbooks, but I just stopped at Boston Chicken and here we are."

"Fine with me," said Brian. "We have this all the time. Mom can't find the energy to cook Monday through Thursday. I love their mashed potatoes."

Mashed potatoes in their plastic bucket were passed first to Brian, followed by chicken, and stuffing, and corn bread.

"Actually," said Janie's father, "I want you to eat fairly quickly, Jodie."

Her parents thought Mr. Johnson was distinguished looking, but to Jodie he was just old and tired.

"You and Brian still have quite a drive ahead of you, Jodie, and you don't want to be on the highway too late. Like any other city," he went on, checking his watch, "Boston can be dangerous."

On the one hand, Jodie appreciated the worry of

grown-ups, but on the other hand, if one more person worried about her one more week, she'd go live in the Antarctic, instead of just Boston.

Janie, wonderfully, defended her sister. "Daddy, Jodie is seventeen. Nearly eighteen. She speaks Japanese. She can parallel park."

Jodie loved it that of all the things she could do, those were the two that impressed her sister.

"And I," put in Brian proudly, "can change a tire."

"What a team," said Mr. Johnson with a smile.

Jodie didn't feel like eating fast. She felt like spending more time here, getting to know them better. Janie on her own turf was so much easier than Janie bristling in New Jersey, afraid of being disloyal to the Johnsons. "Janie," said Jodie suddenly, "why don't you come with us to Boston? It's only for two days. You could cut school tomorrow, you're an A student, and nobody minds you cutting school if it's for college visits."

"Come with you?" Janie found this such an amazing idea, she had trouble finding a place to set her glass down. Mr. and Mrs. Johnson froze in place and tried to reactivate themselves with swallows and blinks.

Janie's not free yet, thought Jodie. We're building our new lives, but Janie hasn't built hers. Maybe her parents need her too much.

"We're staying at the Marriott," said Jodie. "The room has two king beds. You and I'll share one, Janie, and Bri will have the other. It'll be so much fun. Come on. Come with us."

"Oh, Mom!" said Janie, glowing. "Say yes!"

How young we are, thought Jodie, compared to

other teenagers. We're eight-year-olds here, waiting for the parents to decide. Who would we be right now, if Hannah hadn't driven through New Jersey?

Janie turned, laughing, to Jodie. "We can drop in on Reeve, too."

"Unannounced," said Jodie. "We'll catch him with some gorgeous college girl."

"Bring a weapon then," said Janie. "He'll be history."

They had never so completely been sisters. Not the red hair, but the patience of waiting for permission; they were mirrors of each other; they had been formed by parental permission more than any other family they knew.

"She is my sister," said Janie, to bolster an argument that hadn't started.

"Her big sister," added Brian. "Her big, reliable older sister."

Mrs. Johnson nodded minutely with her chin, and Mr. Johnson, appointed spokesman, said, "Okay. You may go to Boston with them."

CHAPTER
EIGHT

Brian knew he had to take the backseat. Jodie and Janie never even thought of discussing seat choices but took the front as their due. The longer you've been on earth, the more front seat you get.

He was glad they'd be seeing Reeve. Reeve was what Brian wanted to be: popular, handsome, tall and at ease.

They'd leave the car in the parking garage at the Marriott. To get around Boston for the next three days, they'd take the T, Boston's trolley-subway system. Brian was desperate to be the kind of person who was comfortable taking the T. Who knew how much a ticket was, and where the routes went, and wasn't afraid of the people who sat next to him.

Plus Boston was the cradle of history. Perhaps he could convince his sisters to go to at least one historic site.

Dream on, thought Brian wistfully.

•   •   •

At WSCK, Reeve took the phones. It was only nine P.M., he could have been in his room studying, but he couldn't stay away. "You've reached WSCK, We're Here, We're Yours, We're Sick, how can I help you?" He loved those lines.

90

"Hi, Reeve. Listen, I just have one question about the janies."

"Just one?" he said. "Normal people have at least a hundred." Reeve disconnected, laughing to himself. He loved how the tip of one finger could remove somebody from his world.

Vinnie said to him, "Remember I had Derek Himself ask for volunteers 'cause we need more disc jockeys?"

Reeve nodded.

"Guess how many people called in?"

"How many?"

"Eleven. Guess how many said they wanted to be just like you? Go overnight from pathetic lame freshman to campus star?"

"Eleven?"

"You're pretty conceited, fella." Vinnie grinned.

The phone lit up. "Hi, you've reached WSCK, We're Here, We're Yours, We're Sick," said Reeve grandly, "how may I help you?"

Vinnie held up ten fingers. Reeve went wild beneath his shrug. Ten people wanted to be Reeve. Eat your heart out, world, thought Reeve. I'm the only one.

"Listen, I just have one question," said the caller in a childish voice. They all said that. Listen, I just have one question.

Listen, I have all the answers, thought Reeve.

• • •

Jodie was telling Janie about the day she and Stephen had gone into New York City thinking they could find Hannah.

"How'd you get away from Mom and Dad?" said

Brian, awestruck. Mom and Dad would *never* have allowed Jodie and Stephen to go into New York City alone.

"We lied," said Jodie, and Brian was thrilled and stunned that his good, decent older sister and his difficult, moody older brother had had this pact between them, this lie, this adventure.

"And did you find her?" said Brian seriously.

"Bri, get a life. How could we find her? There are seven million people in New York City."

"Then what made you look to start with?"

"Remember the police report? She'd been arrested in New York two years before? Of course, back then they didn't know she was the kidnapper, they just thought she was a common hooker, they wouldn't figure out who the kidnapper was until Janie figured it out. Stephen and I thought she might still be in New York, so we went there."

Brian had been to New York with school groups. He hadn't been able to find the Metropolitan Museum, never mind one particular woman out of seven million. He forgot about being so nice to his sisters that they would agree to go to Faneuil Hall with him. "Pretty stupid to think you could find her."

"We felt stupid all day long," Jodie agreed, "but we also felt okay. It's hard to describe. At the end of the day, I didn't want to murder Hannah. Or you either, Janie."

Janie made noises of irritation. "I don't see why you had fantasies of murdering me. I had no choices in this whole thing. And besides, what if you had found Hannah? Nothing could be worse.

Do you realize what we would go through if Hannah appeared? A trial."

It would be Hannah accused in court, but it would be Janie's mother and father who were tried, by television, and radio, and newspapers, and neighbors.

"We'd be on CNN for a year," pointed out Brian. He thought this was cool, but he knew his parents and Janie's parents didn't. They'd die first. Hannah might deserve a trial, but they didn't, and there was no escape once these things began.

Brian thought of himself on the witness stand, being calm and handsome and knowledgeable. Of course, he wouldn't be called. He'd been a toddler in diapers when it had happened. His mother had literally kept the twins on leashes; little harnesses as if they'd been dogs pulling carts. Brian hated to look at photographs of himself on a leash.

How quickly Janie and Jodie left the fascinating topic of Hannah. Brian wanted Janie to talk about what her Johnson parents thought when they thought about Hannah. Were they full of guilt? Anger? Horror? What did they say out loud to the daughter they had acquired by theft?

He listened to his sisters talking, enjoying the plural: two sisters. But they were boring, which was the habit of girls, talking about the personalities of boys instead of anything interesting, so Brian stared out the window instead. Turnpikes at night were like girl talk: not interesting.

●   ●   ●

Jodie was a good driver. They drove north on 395, rural with little traffic, and picked up the Mass

93

Pike, where a steady thrum of trucks pushed them faster and faster toward Boston.

Janie wondered when she would develop a desire to drive. She felt stunted sometimes, as if the discovery of her two families had cut off something essential; kept her a child while everybody around her grew up.

Janie knew suddenly that the Johnsons were all playing house: her mother, her father and her—staying little, staying inside.

She played with the radio dial. Both New York and Boston came in clearly. She loved thinking about Reeve on radio. She loved thinking about Reeve. Boston sounded so romantic. While Jodie was touring colleges, Janie could be with Reeve. She thought of wedding gown fabric: satin, lace, velvet, brocade. She thought of veils and gloves.

She laughed to herself in the dark of the car, but it was no joke. She dreamed of a life with Reeve. In this life, he was not just standing with his arm around her; he had his arms around all the players in this sad game, and she and they loved him for being sturdy. She thought of him in terms of wedding vows: for better or for worse. He had certainly seen her worst, and had waited calmly for her best to return.

One thing she knew. Reeve was sick of calm. He'd like some wild in their relationship.

Janie pretended Reeve was next to her, and she snuggled up to his invisible heat, warming herself on his invisible chest.

• • •

Reeve was tired of gentle janies. He'd rehearsed truly wrenching janies for tonight. It would be his best night. People phoning in would get busy signals.

He waited for ten o'clock.

Derek was offering a prize to the listener who could answer a Boston music trivia question.

Prize.

A phrase Reeve associated with Martin Luther King filtered through his mind. *Keep your eyes on the prize.*

What was that prize, for Reeve?

He did not need freedom. He had too much of it. The prize, for Reeve, was *not* to use his freedom.

The prize is not a million listeners, and money, and fame, thought Reeve. The prize is shutting up.

If he shut up, nobody would hear his really good janies.

Besides, I won't get caught, he told himself.

Anybody who worries about getting caught knows he is wrong. Reeve did not want to think about right and wrong. He just wanted to enjoy his new place in the world. He resented Martin Luther King for appearing in his mind, righteous and judging.

He whispered *prize* to himself, turning the prize back into a pair of Derek's tickets.

• • •

Boston popped out of the ground. They'd been on a boring highway, with boring buildings, they entered a tunnel, and *wham!* There was Boston, skyscrapers and hotels, neon lights and streetlights and office-at-night lights.

Jodie concentrated on being in the correct lane at the correct time, but she never once picked the correct lane, and had to whip between cars and risk fender benders and listen to angry honks.

They hit the Marriott at 10:14.

The place was so efficient that they were in the room at 10:21.

"Reeve broadcasts Thursday nights from ten to eleven," said Janie. "Let's listen to his station."

Brian took over the radio. It was a cheap little thing, brown and black plastic with a sleep alarm, and Brian had trouble finding WSCK. "They're just down the block," said Janie. She tried tuning and got nowhere. Jodie finally managed to get the station, and there was Reeve's voice, big and sexy and deep, announcing Visionary Assassins.

Brian cracked up. "I'd sing in a group with that name."

"Or maybe you wouldn't," said Jodie after listening for a minute. "Visionary Assassins ought to be assassinated for pretending to be a band."

They lay back on their beds, giggling at the ceiling, punchy from having accomplished the trip and being on their own in a wonderful city, with freedom in front of them.

• • •

"Okay, the pressure's on!" cried Derek Himself into the mike. "The interest is up, the calls are in, you guys want another janie tonight. Well, we got a special coming up. A twofer. Along with a couple of janies, Reeve's promised us a hannah."

Reeve flexed his arms, took the mike, felt the

sweep of pleasure rushing from mike to heart. He prepared his best speaking voice, his best timing, his most dramatic pauses.

Janie didn't go politely into being Jennie. She went fighting and spitting.

The courts said Janie had to be returned to her biological family. To New Jersey. Lawyers took her down the same interstate we took the day we skipped school. But this time, it wasn't a road. It was a tunnel of fear. Janie was being poured down some evil tube, where she could land in any kind of nightmare, because she no longer had parents. She was mad at Hannah, she was mad at the world, but mostly she was mad at her birth parents. How dare they want her back, when she liked her old life better?

Janie found out something while she was living in New Jersey. She didn't have enough love to go around. Janie turned out to have a limited supply of love. Not enough to fit in her real mother and father. Who needed them? Janie had a great life. They were clutter.

Reeve felt strangely less cluttered himself. It dawned on him that one reason he was so good at this was because he, too, had ended Janie's terrible year with a heart full of confusion and pain. He, too, needed the release of confession.

97

•   •   •

Janie lay inside her body and turned into plastic. A Barbie doll.

Reeve.

She couldn't pull her lips together to say his name, or any other name, or any other word.

Reeve.

•   •   •

Jodie thought it was a good thing she was not armed. If she'd had a shotgun, or a machete, she would have used it on Reeve Shields.

On the air, that Janie never wanted to be one of us, Jodie thought.

On the air, that Janie went back to her other family because she loved them more.

It would kill my parents.

Jodie felt like a gun going off, friction, powder, explosives, hot as a cannon. She felt white-hot and violent. *I'll kill Reeve.*

Was this how her brother Stephen had felt all those years? Had Stephen been filled with this rage and had to control it? Who could live with this much fury? It was burning up her thinking.

I hate Reeve's filthy guts.

She had to find some degree of control before she attempted speech. Otherwise nothing but swear words and meaningless shrieks would come out of her throat. I'm the oldest, thought Jodie, I have to set an example.

I'll kill him.

•   •   •

Derek introduced the hannah.

Reeve could feel his listeners. It was an incredible hot sensation. He *knew* they were there. Glued, hungry, thirsty.

He was just as glued. He was hungry and thirsty to hear himself.

Who, really, is Hannah? Of course everybody was being kind to her parents, and pretending she was a misguided lost soul . . . but she wasn't. She snatched a baby girl and left that family to worry forever. And that's evil. Hannah was evil.

The families, even the Springs, did not consider Hannah evil. Pathetic. Wrong. Lost. But not evil.

Reeve had learned, however, as all shock jocks before him had learned, that the best topic is always evil.

If you don't have evil, invent it.

If it isn't exciting enough, embellish.

And where is Hannah now?
She's out there.
Somewhere . . . the sweet dishrag daughter . . . the thief of two families . . . is out there.
All grown up.
All evil.

The word *evil* was heavy and coppery in Reeve's mouth. He lingered on the word, so that his audience would taste it.

Then he upped the ante.

Ante.

A card game term. A gambling term.

It meant: If things are exciting now, just you wait. I'll make it more risky. And then we'll see.

Reeve lowered his voice, as if in the privacy between a human and the Almighty, he was offering up a genuine prayer.

Janie had a prayer.
The prayer was not to God.
It was to Hannah.
Dear Hannah, don't show up in our lives. My parents can't go through that. They'd have to see what became of you. And they and you would have to face a trial and the media. Hannah, there's only one thing you can do for the mother and father you abandoned.
Stay lost.

• • •

Horror spread down Janie's body like snakebite. The poison was cold, crawling through her system. It was cold inside her head, too. Air-conditioned nightmare.

Reeve Shields had sold her over the air.

While she had been heartsick over a page in the yearbook, Reeve—*her Reeve*—had been using her as evening entertainment for a whole city. A joke between Assassins.

There was nobody in the world you could trust. Your parents turned out to be somebody else entirely, and the boy you loved, your worst enemy.

• • •

Brian felt older than his sisters. He could be the parent here, the coach or teacher. The designated grown-up.

Janie had melted into the bed. Her face had a flat look, as if she had abandoned it.

Jodie looked like a losing tennis star. Ready to rip the net and bring her tennis racket right down over the head of her opponent and wrap it around his throat and strangle him while she was at it.

Brian stared at his two flaking-out sisters. *Reeve*, he thought. But we all loved you. You made it possible for us to forgive Janie for wanting to be a Johnson instead of a Spring. You were my hero, Reeve.

Brian felt destroyed around the edges. He picked up the telephone. He hit nine to get an outside line. Twice Derek Himself had given the phone number for WSCK. Brian was not usually strong on numbers, but he would never forget these seven.

• • •

Reeve set up two Visionary Assassins back to back. He was very attached to the Assassins.

101

Vinnie was out in the hall talking to somebody Reeve didn't recognize. Derek had actually retreated to another room to study. Cal had a date.

The phone lit. Reeve was as exhausted as if his mind had been vacuumed. Broadcast took a lot out of you. He stared at the silent, visible ring of the phone. Then he picked it up. He was mildly surprised when the tape reel next to him began turning. Derek must have been recording.

"Hi there," he said briskly into the receiver, finding his jock voice for another moment. "WSCK, We're Here, We're Yours, We're Sick. How can I help you?"

The caller was a woman.

Not a girl. Not a college kid. Not young.

The voice was tired. The vocal cords rasped from too much smoking. The speech was slurred, as if the caller had had too much to drink. "This—this is the radio station?" said the caller.

Derek would have said No, this is the high command, give me your latitude and longitude so I can drop a bomb on you. We have too many stupid people in the world.

But Reeve said courteously, "Sure is. What's your name?"

There was a pause, as if the caller needed to think about this, or needed to be prompted. Needed Reeve to say Yes, your airtime has started, the world is listening, go ahead.

And yet, not that kind of pause.

Not a person uncertain about whether it had started.

A person choosing to start something.

"I," said the voice, "am Hannah."

CHAPTER
NINE

Reeve turned to Styrofoam.

Hannah.

No. Absolutely not. It was not probable. Statistics were against it. It was not logical. It was—

It was the worst thing that could happen.

He felt so light. He might float off the chair and tap against walls, a lost object in a space flight.

Hannah.

Vinnie was still in the hall, still talking to the stranger. Not even enough time for a change of posture had passed.

Nobody was paying attention to Reeve.

The reel-to-reel tape, in its slow, old-fashioned way, circled on. It was taping silence now. Neither Reeve nor his caller spoke.

He said to himself: It's not Hannah. It's some college sophomore joking around. It's Cordell paying Pammy to lower her voice.

But could Pammy's high, annoying burble be transformed into that rough smoker-drinker voice?

He tried to calm himself.

It was Visionary Assassins. They'd hired a voice. For the Assassins, the more attention, the better. They, too, could up the ante.

It's giggly girls with nothing else to do. Junior

high kids listening after they're supposed to be in bed. Kids in the student center, sick of video games. The professor's wife, filling in her chart.

But not Hannah.

He felt cold from the inside out.

He needed to swallow and couldn't. He needed to throw up and couldn't. He needed to think and couldn't.

"I need to know one thing," said the voice. "Just one."

They all said that. But this voice shivered on the words. It was not a demand. It was a plea.

Reeve disconnected. With the slightest pressure from just one finger, he got rid of the voice.

Then he stared at the phone. Why did I do that? I know so much that almost nobody else knows. I could have asked a single question myself, and if it's Hannah, or if it's not—I'd know.

She's gone now. I can't ask.

His mouth was full of something. A towel. Probably his tongue.

And what if it is Hannah? What then, stupid? he said to himself. His pulse whacked in his temple. It felt like a golf ball under the skin. Hire a real Visionary Assassin to do away with her? Invite her for dinner? Suggest a friendly local FBI agent?

If it was a listener trying to increase the action, he thought, she'll call back.

He waited. His heart beat as fast as a hummingbird's.

This is a college town, he reminded himself. Boston in November equals bored college kids with nothing better to do than listen to a dumb college radio station and make dumb calls.

104

Around him, clocks with sweep hands ticked off seconds.

Then, once more, the clear plastic bump on the telephone twinkled.

He tried to wet his lips. Couldn't. Tried to look away long enough to find his Coke. Couldn't.

Should he answer?

One more ring and the answering machine would pick up. He could not have Vinnie notice anything amiss.

Vinnie would love it, thought Reeve. He'll make it be Hannah even if she's not Hannah. In fact, Vinnie is the likeliest person to set this up.

His eyes flickered to Vinnie out in the hall. Vinnie was not subtle, could not act. If he was in this, it would show. But Vinnie continued to wave his clipboard at the stranger.

Reeve picked up the phone, finger poised over the Disconnect button. Reeve had large hands: hands meant for circling basketballs or carrying one end of a piano. A voice on a wire had reduced his hand to quivers.

Janie loved his hands. Loved resting her thin fingers against his big ones. He could not think of Janie now. He could not allow himself to think what he might have loosed upon Janie.

It's not Hannah, he repeated to himself. That call was a joke.

And what was selling Janie? he thought. *A joke?*

He had been building a bomb here, as carefully as a terrorist in a basement. And hadn't even realized it.

But who would be blown up?

Not me, he thought. I'm the talk show host. Nothing happens to the host. Hannah isn't my daughter. She isn't my kidnapper. She's theirs.

Reeve managed a swallow. Dry, no Coke.

Hannah would explode Janie, and both families.

It'll go away, Reeve told himself. I didn't really do anything, and nobody really listens to this station. It isn't Hannah, and I'll stop doing janies. I'll attend class, I'll study, eat at McDonald's instead of the cafeteria, pick up my mail in the dark of night, sleep in the park. "This is WSCK! We're Here, We're Yours, We're Sick, how can I help you?" Only his fingers quivered, not his vocal cords.

"I just have one question, Reeve." Chipper, perky voice. Demanding, in a Hills College way. "I wanna know if Visionary Assassins look like their songs. Somebody told me that in real life, they're wimpy, weedy nerds. I picture them as big, lean thugs. What's the truth?"

Reeve's horror faded to nothing. He felt thick and somewhat silly. His racing pulse dropped, and his sweat dried.

"Ah, the elusive truth," said Reeve. "Only if you see the Assassins live will you come close to the truth." He disconnected.

Well, that was a relief. No Hannah. Just an ordinary evening in the life of a deejay.

He'd have to put a third CD on. He couldn't fill his lungs enough to talk on the air. Couldn't wet his lips.

He felt like somebody who's just missed having a fatal car accident and has to pull over until the jelly-legs go away. He took two extremely deep, calming breaths, the way he used to do in high school before a wrestling match.

High school. Talk about remote. He'd been a kid then, with kid-sized problems.

This is a kid-sized problem, too, he reminded himself.

The phone lit once more.

He tried to plan what to say to the fake Hannah, but no plan came to mind. He'd have to wing it. This time he would not hang up. He had to hear the woman out, find out who was behind her nonsense.

"Hey! You've reached WSCK! We're Here, We're Yours, We're Sick, how can I help you?"

"Reeve? This is Brian Spring. Jodie and I are here in Boston for her college interviews. We heard your broadcast."

Reeve had been braced for a fake Hannah. Not a real Brian Spring. Reeve's head splintered. Brian and Jodie? *But they would tell Janie.*

"We're at the Marriott. We're not alone, Reeve. Janie came up with us," said Brian. "The Marriott. Room six sixteen. You better come here."

Janie was here.

Janie had listened.

It felt as if the blood had been siphoned right out of his body.

He had thought Hannah's voice the worst-case scenario.

No. Janie hearing his worst janie was.

An hour ago, Reeve had considered it his best.

•   •   •

The coldness in Janie's system made it hard to think. She was freezing up like an arctic pipeline.

Could she have borne it if Reeve had spilled her to a sympathetic roommate? Maybe.

But he had chosen the world. Radio existed wherever a dial existed. Millions of locations. Millions of listeners.

And so many lies! He was a gofer, he'd said, the new kid on the block, a filer of papers and a sorter of cassettes. Not so.

"I don't want him in this room with me!" Janie shouted at Brian. In times past, when life or truth had threatened, she'd had torrents of weeping, bad dreams, woozy desperation for weeks. Go through that again, without Reeve to lean on? Instead, Reeve to blame it on?

• • •

Jodie found an extra blanket on a shelf and put it over her shivering sister. Janie cocooned in it, rolling up into the wool. Only her hair showed, a frizzy ripple of red at the end of a green cloth tube.

"What do we say to Reeve once he gets here?" asked Brian.

"You're the one who called him," said Janie from inside her muffler. "I'm certainly not going to say anything to him. He sold me! Like he opened a store, and I was the product!"

"You can't breathe like that," said Jodie, yanking the blanket down a little.

I don't feel like breathing, thought Janie.

Jodie flopped down next to her. "But Reeve is

the good guy! I can't understand how he could have done this."

"If somebody told us," said Brian, "we wouldn't believe it. But we heard him."

"Maybe I should call Mom and Dad," said Jodie nervously, getting up off the bed again.

"What?" Brian jumped between her and the phone. "Forget it! We're going to get rid of this, not make it bigger. Bring parents in? Are you crazy?"

"Right," said Jodie, "you're right, Bri, I was crazy."

Yet another enormous horror that I cannot tell my mother and father, thought Janie.

She thought of the tremendous effort she had put into protecting her parents. Her "I'm okay, we're okay, it's okay" stance. She knew as an absolute that neither parent could endure this betrayal.

She would have to bear it.

•   •   •

Reeve had not thought of the janies going down roads, into hotels, inside travelers' cars. The dorms, yes; the student center, the occasional professor's house.

He saw himself as an ignorant fool; somebody who really did not understand the technology behind radio.

It existed. It had a life. Anybody could turn that life on.

The phone at WSCK continued to ring. Three more calls.

His bright, cheery voice identified the station. "How may I help you?" said his very own voice.

They were not Hannah. They were not Brian. They were two janie and one Grateful Dead requests. "We don't do the Dead," Reeve said, "call a commercial station for that."

For the first time since he had begun at WSCK, he wanted the phones to shut up. No more calls. Don't invade me! I have to think.

But I'm not the one who was invaded. Janie was.

He glanced at the air check. He would play back tonight's tape, listen to his janies, so that he could—what? Plan his defense? He didn't have a defense.

He saw the unfolding of this evening. Janie telling her mother and father, who would be sick and shocked and would hate Reeve. The Johnsons telling his own mother and father, who not only would be sick and shocked, but also hold themselves responsible, because they should have brought him up better. He saw Thanksgiving vacation, only days away, during which his excellent sisters and brother would tell him how worthless and disgusting he was. And they'd be right.

"Reeve?" said Derek. His voice was strange. Reeve could not analyze it. "You okay?" said Derek.

It was concern. Derek, who was jealous of him, was concerned.

"I'm fine," said Reeve. He still couldn't focus on the Coke; Derek had to hand it to him. Everything was air. Air talk, airtime, air check, air brain.

"You didn't even log in the last few calls," said Derek.

Reeve's neck bent with difficulty, as if he had a brace on it, and he saw that he had made no entries.

110

There was no record of the Hannah call; no record of Brian.

The person who really counted was Janie, and of Janie there was a record, all right. Weeks and weeks of it.

Courtesy of Reeve.

•   •   •

Brian and Jodie discussed the death penalty, and whether there was something worse and more painful for Reeve to suffer.

Janie lay motionless in the itchy, woolly dark of the blanket.

When she and Reeve were apart, whether for an hour or a month, she got so eager to touch him that when he appeared, she could *not* touch. She would find herself dancing around him. He'd have to touch her first and break the spell.

Oh, Reeve!

She wanted to cry. Tears were both wrenching and comforting. But she was not near crying; she was in some grim, dark place without tears or hope.

This is where my parents are over Hannah, she thought. Hannah's betrayals sent them forever into tearless, hopeless dark.

She saw the years of her parents' suffering, and shrank from it. No, please, don't let it hurt me that long and that badly!

But it would. Because it was Reeve.

Reeve, whose presence was beneath her, around her, with her, supporting her. As if she were a swan, floating on the ocean of Reeve's steadiness.

Oh, Reeve!

What was I to you, in the end?

Is this the end?

Well, of course, it has to be.

The end, she thought, and the two words were horrible and bleak. She had thought the two words would be *I do*. No. The two words were *the end*.

"We don't tell anybody," instructed Brian. "You listening to me in there, Janie? We don't tell anybody."

As if I could tell a soul, thought Janie. As if I could pick up the phone and say, Sarah-Charlotte, guess what?

"What about Brendan?" Jodie asked. "He's your twin."

•   •   •

Brian had not told his twin much in months, and his twin had told him nothing. It no longer ranked as betrayal. Not with Reeve for comparison.

In the midst of his shock over Reeve, Brian felt a great relief about his brother. It was okay to be twins and be different. One was an athlete and one was academic.

Out loud he said, "I don't tell Bren much anymore. And he doesn't have an imagination."

Brian had not known that until his mouth said it, and then he realized that was half the problem. "Brendan doesn't think about us," said Brian. "He won't lie awake at home tonight wondering if he missed something by not coming to Boston."

Home. Brian had an image of people who slept soundly, safe in what they did not know.

Brian would have said that if anybody was safe, it was Reeve.

112

"It makes me think of the leaf-sucker," said Janie.

"Ick," said Jodie. "Some kind of insect? Sucking juice out of leaves?"

"No. In the fall, when the leaves come down . . . beautiful maple leaves, orange and crimson and gold . . . you rake your leaves into the street. The town crew comes by with a leaf-sucker machine, and they suck them up and grind them into tiny, dusty shreds. I hated the leaf-sucker when I was little. It was so scary, all those beautiful leaves, turned into brown shred."

"Yeah, well, you're not brown shred," said Brian, "you're still our sister and Reeve is still—well—"

"Brown shred," said Jodie.

•   •   •

Eleven o'clock must have come, because Vinnie took over the mike.

Reeve sat where he was.

He felt like the carpet on the wall. Thick and gray and stuck with pins.

Vinnie barely glanced at him. He set out the CDs, cassettes and records he was going to play. Then he introduced the next song. Vinnie was inside the mike, unaware that another human being occupied the room with him.

Reeve rewound the tape that recorded call-ins. As easily as that, he was rid of the Hannah voice. It had been taped but not aired, and now it wasn't taped either. It hadn't happened.

He left the building.

City lights cast a pinkish glow upon a cloudy

113

sky. The air was crisp, as if the weather had plans.

I can't face Janie, he thought.

He had to close his eyes against her image, but he knew her so well that the image was within him and did not go away.

She'll hate me, Reeve thought, and the certainty of this stabbed him.

He headed for the T.

I don't have to go to the Marriott, he thought. I could go back to the dorm. And do what? Lie there staring up at Cordell's mattress, knowing Janie's waiting?

When the train came (quickly, which was not fair; you were supposed to wait at night) he thought of riding the car to the end of the line. Getting off wherever that might be and picking up a new life. He thought of trying to explain himself to Janie. Explaining to her parents, and his parents, and the New Jersey parents, and on top of that—*what if it was Hannah?*

It just couldn't be. Surely it was Vinnie. Or Visionary Assassins. Or Pammy. Or the professor's wife.

Or Hannah.

CHAPTER
TEN

The hotel was quiet and undemanding at this hour. Lobby, ferns, palms, flowers, desks. Reeve walked to the distant bank of elevators. Nobody looked his way. He was the wholesome type. People trusted Reeve.

The elevator moved swiftly to the sixth floor.

He had mike fright. The blank horror of his own speech.

Mirrors reflected him too many times. He did not want to look at himself. He kept his eyes on the doors, and when they opened he stepped through. The hotel was thickly carpeted. He walked silently, as if he weren't coming after all.

If only that were true.

He wondered if the excuse that he had needed confession would work; that talking had been good for him.

But the Catholic Church knew what it was doing when it kept confession down to a tiny room with two people. Confession to millions is not the same. Brian and Jodie, good Catholics, were going to cut that argument to pieces pretty fast.

He had planned to stand in the corridor thinking things through before he knocked, but they were waiting. Jodie opened the door and stood

115

back. She was more pixielike than Janie, but the look she gave him was not elfin.

Inside 616 was a little hall painted gum-wrapper green. Past Jodie was a large room with two enormous beds and an enormous television resting on a long bank of drawers. There was an armchair, a round table and a little sofa, the kind called a love seat.

There was Brian, looking very young: more elementary school than junior high. Bobbling around like a kid on a playground ready to fight.

Janie, presumably, was the roll of blanket.

Nobody said anything.

The radio was off. The television was off. They were too high to hear traffic.

My turn, thought Reeve, and he was afraid. "I'm sorry," he said finally.

• • •

There was no fight-or-flight reaction in Brian.

Only fight.

He wanted to slam Reeve to the floor, kick his ribs in, bash his skull. He wanted to hit—bite—kill. It was so primitive, so complete, that Brian's mind didn't have sentences in it; just images.

Brian despised himself for being little, for being short and thin and a crummy athlete. He hated how Reeve's eyes passed over him, ruling him out. He wanted to protect and fight back, not be the little boy watching to see what the big boys did.

But if he attacked, Reeve would just hold him off, and Brian would be pathetic, and the girls would have to waste time separating them, and somehow this would make it easier on Reeve.

116

So Brian stood still, pressing his angry arms against his heaving sides.

· · ·

"You sold us!" said Jodie. "You took our story, the hard parts, the insider stuff, the things that hurt most, and you sold it."

"I'm sorry," said Reeve again. He was sorry. He was horribly sorry.

"You didn't think you'd get caught, did you?" said Jodie.

"No."

Janie's hair had spilled out of the blanket tube. If only he could fling the blanket off Janie, and tighten his arms around her, and muss up her hair, and convince her that he really was a good guy. A mistake, sure, but hey. Shrug it off, Janie.

"How could you do it, Reeve?" screamed Jodie without raising her voice; a scream of intensity, not volume. "How could you actually say things like Janie not wanting us? Janie not having enough love to go around? Bad enough to mention what people already know from newspaper and television. But to tell what we kept safe in our hearts? How could you do that to us?"

The word *safe* and the word *heart* were terrible. "It didn't feel real," he said. "It was just airtime. It's just you and the mike. You're alone in a glass room and it isn't real."

She shook her head. "I don't buy that. We're radio fiends, too. The first thing in radio is to hook the listeners. You knew the audience was out there. You were buying listeners, Reeve."

He swallowed. "Yes."

"Buying them through me," said Janie.

Her voice jolted him terribly. It was still her voice. She's still who she was, he thought confusedly. A lump in his throat like broken pavement blocked speech.

"For fame?" said Jodie. "Was this part of your master plan to be rich and famous?"

"I guess so," he said. Janie did not move inside the blanket; she could have been dead. He said to the blanket, "Radio is exciting. It's live. People recognize your voice, and they call up the station and ask for you, and you have automatic friends. Strangers smile when they meet you." But Janie, he thought, Janie isn't going to smile when she meets me. Oh, God.

"If you did it so people would know you, why didn't you talk about yourself instead? The freshman experience or something?" said Jodie.

"Because I started so early," said Reeve. "I'd hardly even been a freshman when I began."

"You've been talking about us since *August*?" hissed Jodie. "How many of these little stories have you woven? How many nights a week? How many details? How many times?"

He could not answer that. It was too damning. He took refuge in his first sentence. "I'm sorry."

He looked at the misshapen blanket that contained the person who mattered most to him in the world. He sat heavily down on the bed, the way he always sat, letting go completely, so that the springs touched bottom.

He peeled the blanket down, and Janie's tired

118

eyes stared back at him. "I'm sorry," he said, "I didn't mean to. I was just being stupid."

• • •

It was Jodie who began to bawl.

Brian's sister was not given to tears; she was battle-prone, and often damaged her brothers. Jodie sobbing made Brian feel uneven, tippy. Wishing they had called Mom and Dad after all.

Brian felt defused. He had expected a monster. But Reeve was still Reeve. The same endearing, good-looking, nice person. The need to damage Reeve faded. Brian just felt mixed up, with a headache on the side.

"We were getting there!" Jodie cried. She was mad at herself for crying, wiping tears away as fast as they fell. "You wouldn't even know my mother and father if you came down. They're happy. They're not worrying. They can let go of us. And look what you did. Threw us out there, like raw meat in front of wolves. Saying on the air that Janie had better things to do than make an effort to love us."

Reeve didn't defend himself.

"You've ruined Boston for me. How am I supposed to get excited about attending school in a town where they know private, personal family hurts?"

Reeve tried to explain how it had begun, how it had snowballed. He described the first night, the agony of having nothing to say. How Derek and Vinnie and Cal were going to laugh at him, along with his entire dorm.

119

Brian hated it that Reeve was a coward. Afraid of being a jerk for five minutes in front of some other jerks? That gave him the right to sell out the family?

"But I never used last names," said Reeve. "I never said Johnson or Spring. So it matters less than you think."

"It doesn't matter *less*, Reeve!" shouted Jodie. "It matters all the way, through and through!"

"People never called in and asked for last names?" said Brian.

"Constantly. That was the point. Make them call in."

"Don't you pretend to yourself or us that you didn't have a choice, Reeve Shields!" Jodie was going to hit him. Brian wondered what Reeve would do. "I don't care how it snowballed. You're a big boy, Reeve, you could have stepped aside and let the snowball go past."

Reeve swallowed. "That's true."

"So what's your excuse?" shouted Jodie.

"I don't have one!" At last Reeve's voice was as strained as Jodie's. Brian was glad to hear the radio richness gone and the ragged nerves showing.

"I was in love with the sound of my voice, I guess. In love with being important. Daydreaming about how famous I would be."

His eyes were still on Janie, and he had a puppy look, with that moppy hair, and Brian thought, If Janie tells him it's okay, she loves him anyway, not to worry about it, then Stephen is right, let her sleep in a coffin.

"I want you to promise me," said Janie, sliding off the bed, keeping it between herself and Reeve,

120

keeping the blanket on, "that you will never say another sentence about us."

Reeve didn't get up. He sat hunched and sagging on his side of the room. "I promise."

"You will never use us on any radio station ever again."

"I promise."

Brian had never heard Janie say *us* before. *Us* meaning her real family.

"Did I hear the announcer correctly?" said Janie. "Did he refer to me as a thing? A janie?"

Reeve closed his eyes.

Coward, thought Brian.

Brian wanted Reeve still to be his hero. He wanted Reeve still to be tall and wonderful and good at everything. We'll have to keep this a secret from Stephen, too, thought Brian, and he imagined hearing Stephen speak highly of Reeve at holidays.

• • •

Janie envied Jodie's tears. She, Janie, was blank; a computer disk that has not been formatted.

Reeve looked so miserable. He was ashamed, she believed that. But his protests were another lie. He had known what he was doing.

No, thought Janie. You said to yourself: Oh well, it's only Janie, but a radio career is a radio career.

She felt soggy, like a swamp.

She thought of her Barbies, how firm they were, how solid and unchanging. If only life could be like that.

But my life is like that. My mother and father and I—we work each day to be as solid and unchanging as dolls. This is what it is to be a doll. Somebody plays with you, and throws you down at the end of the day.

"Janie," whispered Reeve, and he moved toward her, and she shook her head, and he stopped.

She tightened the blanket around herself. She could not imagine ever coming out from under the blanket.

• • •

Reeve was sick from knowing himself.

Janie had felt her way to the armchair. The beautiful hair seemed unconnected to her: It belonged to somebody who danced and laughed.

"There's one more thing," said Brian. "This is a secret, Reeve. Even though you've told all Massachusetts, it's a secret. We don't tell any of our parents."

"Yeah, Reeve, we let the parents go on thinking you're a nice person," said Jodie.

"We don't tell Stephen," said Brian, "we don't tell Sarah-Charlotte, we don't discuss your radio show again. Ever."

I sure don't want them to know either, thought Reeve drearily. "What about your twin?" he asked Brian. "You tell him everything, don't you?"

"No, Reeve," said Brian quietly. "You're the one here who tells everything."

Reeve flushed.

Janie had looked up. Reeve could not meet Janie's gaze. There was something glinting about her, like a setting sun in his eyes. Without inflection, just plain words, as if reading a vocabulary

122

list, Janie said to him, "Don't call me. Don't come to my house when you're home."

"No, Janie, please," he said, and his voice cracked. "I still love you. Let me talk to you alone. Please."

"If you even *liked* me, you would have stopped yourself from doing this."

"That's not true. I just wasn't thinking. I still love you."

"Oh, shut up," said Jodie. "We hate you, so it's hate, so shut up and leave."

Janie tightened the blanket, insulating herself.

Brian put a light hand on Reeve's sleeve and guided him out; out of the room, into the hall, onto the thick carpet; and then Brian shut the door and Reeve was alone in the hotel corridor. He could hear the *ding* of arriving elevators and a cluttery rush of ice cubes falling in their machine.

I've raped Janie, thought Reeve.

That's what talk shows are. The rape of the soul.

CHAPTER
ELEVEN

Boston.

One A.M.

A thin, mean rain was coming down.

The T was closed. Reeve had no cash for a taxi. He walked.

Even at this hour, in this weather, he was not the only person on the streets. Well-dressed people emerged from bars, drunks slept in doorways, police cruised in cop cars. Scrungy little convenience stores were full of light and customers.

He could not go to his dorm. He didn't even want to think about the thoughts he would have, trying to sleep.

The next block was deserted. He found himself slinking through the shadows at the edges of buildings, instead of striding down the sidewalk. He was a thing that needed to stay hidden.

Was this how Hannah had felt, when she made the final error, the ultimate betrayal of her upbringing, and became a kidnapper? Hannah, hiding in her parents' home with little Jennie Spring, telling them monumental lies: Did she know she had become part of the dark?

Why was she calling WSCK?

Is any spotlight better than the dark? Even the spotlight of arrest and trial and imprisonment?

Reeve corrected himself. It was not, it could not be, Hannah.

In his head, he replayed the Hannah call. From the inflection in that voice, he tried to get a picture of what the woman looked like.

Radio was words. The listener had to supply the rest. The only photos of Hannah were from high school, so it was easy to think of her as a young, thin dishwater blond, head down, not making eye contact even on the yearbook page.

The big question was still the question with which Reeve had opened his show: *Now what?*

This is where we came in, Reeve's listeners would say.

He was exhausted. His knees wanted to quit. Reeve leaned against a building and slid down the bricks to the sidewalk, like a drunk. The expression on Janie's face! The stunned blankness, as if he had slapped her. I did slap her, he thought.

His heart wanted to quit.

Now what?

• • •

Brian was only thirteen. He was asleep by one A.M. Jodie, having driven from southern New Jersey, was even more tired, and she too fell asleep.

Only Janie was awake in the night, in the dark.

She stayed in the armchair. The drapes were open, and she looked out on a sliver of the city. It was a hard, building-edged slice, like an architectural drawing, yellow at the edges from the glow of streetlamps.

It came to Janie Johnson that Reeve Shields

125

was a soft person from a soft world. When he ran into a hard decision, he made a soft one.

Whereas she, and Jodie, and even Brian—age thirteen—were hard, because theirs had been a hard world; and when they ran into hard decisions, they knew how to make a hard choice.

How wrong that Reeve, her Reeve, was soft.

He was physically stronger, taller, broader. He was all the good things, from handsome to fine company.

And soft.

I still love you, he had claimed. But love should make a person step back and think again. She no longer knew what love was. Or who Reeve was.

Maybe, she told herself, he just hasn't grown up yet.

No. Because Brian's grown up, and he's only thirteen.

She felt such pain through her heart that she did not know if she could live through it. But she had had pain before, and she knew that you did come out on the other side. You were not necessarily happier or better for it. But you arrived in another place.

I don't want some other place. I want Reeve the way he was.

She watched Jodie and Brian breathing. She had to believe that some people were as steady and reliable as breathing.

But who?

• • •

Boston.

Two A.M.

126

WSCK broadcast around the clock. Hanging out at the station beat going back to his dorm, so Reeve entered WSCK.

He was as surprised to see Vinnie as Vinnie was to see him. This hour was for new guys, for slaves. Vinnie knew something was wrong when Reeve appeared. Vinnie wouldn't care what was wrong unless it affected the station. People were welcome to have all the nervous breakdowns they wanted, just not on Vinnie's time. So Reeve said, "Couldn't sleep."

Vinnie shrugged. People's health problems did not interest him. "Want to introduce you," said Vinnie. He waved forward two guys and a young woman. "This is Reeve, the guy whose program made you decide to show up here at two in the morning."

They beamed at Reeve. "Hi, I'm Cathy!" said the girl. "I love your janies. WSCK sounded so fun. I wanted to do it so bad. Vinnie's not a real fan of women, so it wasn't easy getting on the future deejay list."

Reeve was not able to banter. "Great to have you aboard," he said lamely. He slouched against the far wall.

"Over here," Vinnie said to the new volunteers, "is the air check. This tape comes on automatically when the mike is on, so it doesn't record music, but it does record everything the jock says." He grinned suddenly. "We got all the janies on tape," he said, waving in the general direction of the messiest shelves. Vinnie was breathy and excited, like at the end of a tense game, when the score could go either way.

127

Reeve's anxiety rocketed.

"We're gonna sell 'em," confided Vinnie. "Syndicate the janies to a hundred radio stations, like Rush Limbaugh or Howard Stern or Imus. I'm gonna assign one of you new guys to go through the tapes, ignore the crap on 'em, and make a single tape of the janies."

A leg cramp seized Reeve. His leg yanked upward, muscles screaming. He doubled over, massaging the kink, and sank down neatly, as if he'd meant to sit on the floor. The pain left him breathless.

Once again, he had forgotten the very technology he loved.

A tape was a collection. It had substance and life.

Promising not to do another janie did not get rid of the janies that already existed.

Vinnie and the new crew went into Vinnie's office. Reeve stood. Pins and needles attacked his leg. He managed to shift his weight and cross the tiny room. Calling on his leg not to be a traitor, Reeve squatted down and tilted his head to check the dates on tapes.

". . . and you've been listening to WSCK!" said the deejay, the same old lines full of the same old exclamation points.

In typical sloppy WSCK fashion, some tapes weren't labeled or were labeled partially. He stacked those from Tuesday or Thursday evening, and checked a wall calendar to see what dates he might have missed.

Vinnie came back in with his troops.

Kicked under a shelf was somebody's old book bag.

"Now these are sliders," said Vinnie, waving at the board. "Watch the deejay."

Reeve loaded the book bag. Eight-inch tapes were cumbersome. He buckled the closures and slung the book bag loosely over his shoulder. Then he turned slowly.

All three volunteers were watching him. "Have a nice night," he said brightly, moving toward the door.

Vinnie gave him a look. He despised people who wished you a nice day, a nice night or a nice weekend.

"Bye, Reeve," said Cathy.

He wondered what she had seen. Would she ask Vinnie why Reeve had taken those tapes with him?

He shut the heavy glass door firmly behind him, taking measured steps up the stairs. His heart was pounding.

Come on, he said to himself. What's Vinnie going to do to me? Give me a lower grade in Disc Jockey 101?

FCC rules required these tapes, but college stations tended to be rickety. Reeve doubted any official would ever check, and if they did, so what?

We're volunteers, he reminded himself, what can they do to a volunteer?

Vinnie will hate my guts. He'll go ballistic, he'll say I stole station property. How am I going to come back here next Tuesday? By then these new guys will have discovered half those tapes are missing, and they'll know it has to be me—and then I say, Oh, even though you have the highest ratings and the highest hopes of your radio life, Vinnie, I'm quitting; no more janies; but I still want

129

to answer the phone. I'm expecting a call, see, and I want to be the one to pick up.

Vinnie would be sorry they didn't broadcast from a higher floor so that he'd have a window to throw Reeve out of.

The rain had stopped, and the wind had turned bitter. Reeve stood under a dark sky and stared at buildings in which thousands of kids his own age slept.

What explanation do I give for not being on the radio anymore? Oh, grow up! he thought, despising himself even more. You don't owe explanations. Just stop.

Hills College lay between neighborhoods where you'd like to spend your life and neighborhoods where you'd rather die first. The streets were scary in their emptiness, but scarier in the fullness of shadows. He walked half a mile to the bridge over the Charles River.

The bridge had a pedestrian corridor. He walked to the center.

One by one, he flipped the tapes like Frisbees into the water.

Oh, Janie, he thought. This time last year, I was buying you a Thanksgiving present. Last year I bought you presents for every holiday. New Year's, Valentine's, St. Patrick's.

Well, this time he had given her something she could really remember him by.

Don't call me. Don't come to my house when you're home.

The last tape slid into the water without a splash.

There, he told himself, trying to believe this had

accomplished something. The janies are gone. Destroyed.

He found himself rolling the empty book bag tighter and tighter, strangling the canvas. *All I have to do now is wonder if I've brought Hannah to life.*

How long would he have to wait before he could feel safe?

A month, a year, a decade?

Does a secret have a life span?

And if so, whose?

Reeve rested his cheek against the cold metal of the bridge, letting it lower his fever. He soothed himself with probabilities.

Almost Thanksgiving vacation. After that, only two weeks of school, during which final exams would take over. Then vacation from December fourteenth till January twentieth.

College kids had too much to think about to remember the janies that long. There was probably citywide attention deficit disorder. Two hundred fifty thousand students busily forgetting everything. People would have transferred and moved and broken up. Nobody would remember last year's drivel on a pathetic little radio station.

So it's okay. I threw the tapes in the river, they're history, it's going to vanish and be okay.

He found himself laughing nervously. A frilly sound. A skirt of ridiculous laughter. He felt like a trapped President in a bad movie.

He could destroy all the tapes in all the radio stations in Boston . . . and if that voice was Hannah, and if Hannah decided she wanted airtime, somebody else would give it to her.

He had no control.

For the first time in his life, he was standing in the middle of a situation that would do whatever it wanted.

CHAPTER
TWELVE

Jodie canceled her Hills College interview but decided to keep the afternoon appointment at Simmons. So after breakfast—a public breakfast, in the hotel restaurant: starched, heavy napkins folded like pyramids, with waiters pouring coffee and bringing expensive toast—they went out of the hotel and stood in the pale November sun.

"Well, we're here," said Brian. "Let's make use of Boston. Let's walk to the Old State House, where the Declaration of Independence was read in July 1776."

Janie and Jodie looked at him as if he were an out-of-date computer chip.

But in the end, they agreed, because they had to do something.

Brian enjoyed Boston. It was not skyscrapery and overpowering. It was a friendly, low-ceiling kind of place. In such a city, surely a mere radio program would be absorbed, fall between cracks, blend with the rest of Boston's violent history.

"I didn't want to go to Hills College anyway," said Jodie, in the tone of voice that informed Brian she had been daydreaming exclusively of Hills. "It doesn't have enough campus. I want grass and a quadrangle and trees to study under."

"I wonder if people really study under trees," said Brian. "You see it in the photographs in college catalogs, but I don't think real life people cry Aha! A tree! Let's study!"

• • •

Janie had studied beneath a tree with Reeve.

Raked leaves with Reeve.

She knew the buttons on his sweater and the whorls of his fingerprints.

Why had he not remembered these things? Or had he remembered, but they didn't mean much?

They meant the world to me, Reeve, thought Janie.

She knew then that she would have to box up her love for Reeve. She wanted to keep it, like a rose from a corsage.

Brian put his hand in front of her, to keep her from stepping off the curb into traffic; the world was thoughtlessly going on without her.

How much discipline do I have? she thought. Can I loathe Reeve in the present, but still love him in the past? It doesn't work in divorce.

She wished she really were a Barbie. Plastic was good, paper was good. Hair and clothes were good. But hearts . . . what good were they?

Jodie, Brian and Janie waited for a walk light, as if they had a place to go and a reason to cross. A car radio blared so loudly that the percussion seemed to be right on the sidewalk with them.

Radio.

Janie listened to radio for music, but Sarah-Charlotte loved talk shows. She used to play talk show the way other little girls played house.

Sarah-Charlotte. The best friend who knew nothing.

Janie's head ached with thoughts of Sarah-Charlotte. Sarah-Charlotte continued to grow up, to acquire poise and depth, whereas she, Janie, seemed to get younger. She would not mature from this experience, she would weaken. And so would her friendship with Sarah-Charlotte weaken, because there would be more secrets than sharing.

Her feet walked.

Her ears heard Brian and Jodie speak.

Sarah-Charlotte was wrong.

Not much was fight or flight.

It was plain old hanging on that mattered.

• • •

They ended up at the Old Corner Bookstore, which Brian had read about in a tour guide to Boston. "Longfellow and Hawthorne and Oliver Wendell Holmes used to read here. Let's go in." Brian nudged the girls until they obeyed.

It was a regular bookstore, less history-minded than Brian had expected. In fact, the local history shelves were quite manageable. I'll buy one book, he thought. This will get me launched in actual reading. Out of the zillions of choices, I'll find one here.

Brian picked out *Paul Revere and the World He Lived In*. It was thick and somehow exciting, with its chapter headings and scholarly notes and bibliography.

Jodie and Janie eyed his purchase. "When did you decide to be a historian?" said Janie.

Brian was relieved to hear her speak at last.

"I've always been a closet historian. I was just keeping up with Brendan for a few years before I came out."

Janie smiled. "What will Brendan do to you when he finds out?"

Brian wanted to hug her smile, he was so glad she could still produce it. "I'm hoping to get points for being his twin," said Brian, "but he'll probably be ashamed to be seen in public with me. I'll be carrying a book and it won't be Stephen King."

"You could put a fake wrapper on it," suggested Janie. "We can hide Paul Revere inside *Pet Sematary*."

"I'm impressed, Janie," said Jodie. "Joking, after last night?"

"I don't think it's me. I think it's my other self."

Jodie nodded. "I've always wondered if everybody has a twin inside. Brian and Bren really became twins, but some of us don't; we just carry the other self around."

"Whoa!" said Janie. "That's a little spooky for me."

For me, too, thought Brian. And believe me, my twin is not my other self.

"I didn't mean I really have another personality." Janie paused to consider what she did mean. "I mean that I can be stronger if I have to be."

They walked on brick sidewalks and slate sidewalks, cracked sidewalks and cobblestones.

Brian read aloud from *Paul Revere and the World He Lived In*. "There were heroes then," said Brian. "Now there are just sleazy people being sleazy on the radio."

They were silent with their thoughts. Who—anytime under the sun—would have thought Reeve could fall under the heading of sleazy?

They got directions for taking the T to Simmons College for Jodie's interview. "Why am I going on this interview, anyway?" said Jodie.

"So you have something to tell Mom and Dad," said Janie. "So you don't have to lie about everything when Mom and Dad ask how Boston went."

A siren screamed. Traffic did not move over for it.

"Janie?" said Brian, trying to be casual. But oh! how this question mattered. "You meant our mom and dad, didn't you?"

Lights changed. Red was gone. Green shone.

And for Brian, Janie changed. She looked amazed, and uncertain, and finally—glad. "Yes, I meant *ours*," said Janie, and she stepped back from Brian and Jodie as if she thought they might refuse this.

Brian's chest tightened. Surely he could tell his mother that, without giving away the Reeve part.

"My mom, my mom, my dad, my dad," said Janie.

Equal, thought Brian. Could she mean that? Could *we* mean that? Can *we* set aside knowing that we were just clutter?

The lights changed again, and they stayed on the corner, and to Brian it was an intersection of life, not traffic; he studied the rushing cars and wondered why they didn't collide more, since in life you were always colliding with everything.

"They have enough to worry about, all my parents," said Janie. "They think everything is okay. And so we're going to leave them at the okay stage."

Jodie took her sister's hand, and Brian had the funniest idea that she was going to kiss it. But of course she didn't. She said, "Sounds like a Western. Leaving on the Okay Stage."

CHAPTER
THIRTEEN

"Did you have a lovely time, darling?" said Janie's mother, scrunching Janie up against her. "I thought of you all weekend," her mother said happily. "How's Reeve? How's Boston? How were Jodie and Brian? Wasn't it wonderful they asked you along? Don't you feel like a country that's had bad international relations, and now they're normalizing? We can normalize with the Springs."

The Okay Stage was not going to be an easy ride.

Because her parents were not okay to start with. Janie loved them: loved them so completely that within her love was pity.

Janie gave her mother another hug to buy time. That, too, was awful—using a hug to hide in. Janie ached to tell her mother about rotten Reeve. But she put her parents first. She hated Reeve right then, for putting himself first. She schooled her face, to keep rage off it. She had not expected rage in herself. *I hate him!* she thought.

"Boston was fabulous. We walked and walked. Brian had read up on everything and knew exactly where we should go, and was full of history." Janie busied herself with coming-in-the-door activities: hanging up the heavy coat, folding the scarf, shelving the gloves, taking off the boots. She was so fiercely angry that when she had the boots off, she wanted to beat the walls with them. Dent the whole house with those heels.

My parents never asked me to grow up, she thought. Is it fair for me to ask them to grow up? Or do I just go on by myself?

Truly, the last thing on earth Janie wanted to do was to go on by herself.

She set the two boots neatly next to each other.

"Brian's a sweet boy," said Janie's mother. "What's the story between Brian and Brendan?"

"Brendan is athletic and Brian's not."

"That's it? That's the whole story?"

Janie did not want a conversation about anybody's whole story.

People didn't deserve to have their whole stories told.

"Hi, kitten," said her father, coming in and pretending to box with her. He was having a snack and handed her a corner of cake, cold from the refrigerator. A refrigerator from which Reeve had probably taken as many snacks as Janie over the years. She wanted to slam Reeve's finger in the door. No. That wouldn't even bruise him. A host of good ideas came to her, like a violent movie: the ways in which she would see that Reeve found out what it was like to get hurt.

"We missed you," said her father. "Three whole days! I hope Boston was worth it." He wore a wheat-colored turtleneck with an oatmeal wool blazer. He looked like a prep school dean.

Down in New Jersey, her other father would have on navy sweats, and whoever hugged him

140

would be scraped by his beard. I love them both, she thought.

The sentence was incredible.

I love them both.

Her rage drained away.

If that was true, if she had come at last to the place where she could love both sets of parents, then yes. Boston was worth it.

"Hi, Daddy," she said, struggling to speak over the lump in her throat. She managed a couple of college campus stories and then retreated to her bedroom and the privacy she desperately needed.

"That's interesting," she heard her father say. "No mention of Reeve. I wonder if that's going to peter out now that he's in college."

It didn't peter out, thought Janie. It crashed.

She closed her door, and nothing got better. She had actually thought that once she was alone in her own room, things would be better.

Oh, Reeve! Why? To be popular? But you've always been popular! You're the kind of guy everybody likes on sight and likes even better once they get to know you. How could you have needed *more* popularity?

Perhaps you can get greedy for popularity, she thought, the way people get greedy for money. Perhaps it's like a slot machine. One taste of being important and you go on and on, throwing your quarters in, greedy for more.

Boston had been worth it.

But to learn that Reeve—her beloved, perfect Reeve—was not worth it . . .

She had never wanted to learn that.

• • •

"Tell us all about Boston!" said Mr. Spring eagerly. The family was in the new kitchen, sitting on pale pine stools. The semicircle of white counter was big enough that they could leave the Sunday newspaper spread out and still serve dinner comfortably.

They were having spaghetti and meatballs. Jodie was a spoon-whirler; Brendan was a slurper; Mom was a cutter; Dad was a masher. Brian could not combine spaghetti with anxiety, so he was not eating at all. Nobody noticed.

"You should have stayed home and come to my games," said Brendan. "They were really exciting." Brendan told them about his games.

What had happened to the silent communication between twins? Brian wanted to know. He might as well have been a plate of meatballs for all Brendan was tuning in.

Discussion of Brendan's success lasted until the salad. Brian was not fond of lettuce. It seemed to Brian his mother should have picked up on this during the past thirteen years, but no, night after night, there was lettuce.

Mom and Dad faced Jodie eagerly. They spoke at the same time. "Is Boston a great town?" asked their mother. "I always thought it would be."

"Which college did you like best, Jo?" said their father.

Jodie shifted herself around. She had to have her entire body in place before she could talk about important things. "I liked them all," she began.

Brendan, however, interrupted to announce

142

what college he would go to and what athletic scholarships he would get.

Brian actively disliked his twin. He wanted to push Brendan's face into his spaghetti.

"You think you'll apply to any of the Boston schools, Jodie?" asked their mother. "You were right, we don't have much time. You have to get applications out by the first of the year."

Boy, when these guys set aside worry, they really did it. Mom and Dad weren't aware of anything wrong. Brian was offended. *Somebody* should be asking what had happened to his appetite.

Jodie did see that her brother had eaten nothing, and she was envious of his good judgment. She was sorry she'd eaten so much. The meatballs had been an especially bad choice. She was heartsick about Reeve; she was eager for college; but college was damaged; she was thrilled about her new sisterhood with Janie; she was worried whether Janie could hold together. These combined like indigestion

After the required college and Boston discussions, Jodie said, "We had a great time with Janie. Mom, she was really a sister. Maybe it was the car, you know? In a car you're so close, and it's so easy to talk."

"That's wonderful!" Mom was beaming.

There, thought Jodie. That's as close as I can get to letting Mom and Dad know that Janie cares about her mom, her mom, her dad, her dad. Any closer and I'd have to touch Reeve.

"You know what, Mom?" said Brian, throwing away his oil-and-vinegar-stained lettuce and moving on to Mrs. Smith's Apple Pie. "With Janie? At the hotel?"

Jodie eyed him tensely. There were no good hotel stories to relate.

"You pulled it off, Mom. We really have been protected. I mean . . . I was thinking . . . seeing her . . . that nothing damaged us. You loved us. You were there." He struggled with what he wanted to say. "But Janie—even with four parents to guard her from harm—Janie gets slugged every time she turns around."

"What do you mean?" said his father. "What happened to Janie now?" Child in trouble. Instant anxiety. Brian was pleased that his father could still get uptight about one of his kids.

"She and Reeve are having problems," said Jodie.

"Is that all," said their father. "Okay with me. They were way too close for my taste."

Jodie glared at her pie wedge. She would have given anything to be that close to a boy. What was with parents? Always insisting that you could be popular, but the minute you got popular, you were "way too close."

"Do you think Janie would come down for Thanksgiving?" asked Mom.

"Not Thursday," said Jodie. "But I bet Friday and Saturday she would. I'll call her tonight and ask."

Jodie was tempted to phone Stephen.

She was desperate to hear her brother's voice. Somebody who knew anger so well could tell her how to be angry, or how not to be so angry. But

Stephen had found safety in a distant place, and Jodie owed him that privilege. Stephen should not have to carry the kidnapped sister burden any longer.

Janie was not making her Johnson mother and father carry the burden either but was carrying it herself.

Jodie helped clean up the kitchen. A little slave labor to go along with the new house would be ideal. Finally she got up to her room. She sprawled on her bed, loving the silence and the space of it. Then she phoned Connecticut.

"Jodie, he called me," said her sister instantly. "He's called three times."

"Reeve has? Too bad you can't electrocute a guy through the phone line."

"I was so glad to hear his voice."

"No! Did you make up with him? I'll kill you."

"I hung up on him, but I was still glad to hear his voice."

"He does have a great voice," admitted Jodie. "Of course after we stick a knife through his ribs and puncture his lungs, he won't." She wasn't sure Janie even heard this contribution. Janie needed to talk.

In fact, Jodie hardly spoke again. From her sister poured out fury and pain and love and sorrow. Reeve's voice had tipped her past control. Jodie was surprised that Janie had not said all these things to Reeve. Then she realized that Janie *had* said all these things to Reeve, all during the previous year.

No wonder Reeve sold it, thought Jodie. Pure agony, all raw—and all fascinating. If you were the kind of person who believes other people are just material—boy, is this ever material!

"Reeve knew I was trying so hard to do the right thing," said Janie, "and the right thing was so hard to figure out, Jodie, because every choice was only *half* right. I kept looking for *whole* right. And then he sells it. Without blinking. I can't decide if he's a rattlesnake, or just a turkey."

Janie needs me, thought Jodie. It took the betrayal of her boyfriend to make that happen.

Janie's Call Waiting beep sounded.

"If it's Sarah-Charlotte, tell her you're busy," instructed Jodie.

• • •

But it was Reeve.

Even hoarse with misery, his voice was beautiful. Janie hated him for not being a person who matched his voice. "Jodie and I were just saying that you're either a rattlesnake or a turkey."

"Turkey," said Reeve. "Janie, please, I'm having a hard time, too. I'm trying to—"

"How dare you ask me for sympathy? Reeve, don't call me again." Janie thought of all the nights she had prayed for the opposite: Please, God, let cute Reeve next door think of me and call.

"Who else am I going to call? Janie, please. Over Thanksgiving weekend, we have to talk."

"There's nothing to say."

"Janie, there is. I've thought so much about what I chose to do, and tomorrow I have to face the guys at the station and let them know that I'm through, and if I could just talk to you—"

146

"No. It hurts me. Stop hurting me." Janie hung up.

The chilly white of her bedroom was not comforting. She wished she still had the room of her childhood.

She wished she still had her childhood.

She clicked back to Jodie, and wondered who she would have been if Hannah had never coaxed her into a stolen car.

CHAPTER
FOURTEEN

Monday morning.

Bleak and gray and wet and raw. Reeve felt the same. The only thing November had going for it was the upcoming family holiday. A holiday Reeve decided to skip.

His mother was shocked. "But Reeve," she said, trying not to cry, "Todd is coming home. We're going to meet his fiancée. Heather. You'll be your brother's best man at their wedding. You have to come home and meet Heather. And Megan and Lizzie both managed time off. The whole family will be here. You have to be home!"

He was still sick with knowing himself. *Mom, I can't visit. What if you find out what kind of person I really am? It's bad enough that I found out. I want to see Janie more than anything, but I don't want that meeting to happen in front of you.*

"Mom, I've made friends up here, and I've been invited to spend Thanksgiving in"—he thought for a moment—"northern New Hampshire, and—uh—it sounds like fun."

One of the more annoying things about his mother was that she had brought up four children. Therefore she was an excellent guesser. "Miranda Johnson told me Janie was in Boston for the week-

148

end with the Spring children and hasn't mentioned seeing you. Did you have a fight with Janie? Are you worried about running into her?"

Reeve couldn't think of a denial fast enough.

"I'm glad," said his mother. "You two have been far too serious. This is good. You'll both branch out, meet other people. You need to date girls in Boston and she needs to date boys here in town. I'm sure it will hurt for a while, but you'll get over it. It's for the best. Take the Wednesday evening train, Lizzie will pick you up."

• • •

The radio station was like a firehouse, or a neighborhood bar. People who loved WSCK showed up to talk, watch each other in action, do the gritty paperwork that was miserable when you had to do it alone but fun when you had company.

Vinnie did not seem to have been informed that tapes were missing. Perhaps he had not been serious about syndicating the janies, or perhaps he hadn't gotten to it yet.

"Can we go into your office, Vin?" said Reeve.

Vinnie's hard eyes bored into Reeve. Vinnie had become bald while still in his teens. His personality was like his skull: undecorated by anything soft like hair. "No," said Vinnie.

Okay, fine. He'd say it here, with Derek and Cal and the new crew milling around. "I'm not going to be able to come back to the station after Thanksgiving."

He had their attention now. He tried not to look at anybody but Vinnie. "I'm not doing well with my studies."

149

"Possibly because you're not studying," said Vinnie. "What does that have to do with WSCK?"

"My parents are on my case."

"So what?" Vinnie's gaze was short and hard. Vinnie was as bad as Reeve's mother. "Janie found out," he guessed.

Reeve looked down and breathed deeply.

"She didn't kill you?" said Derek, interested. "I would have."

"She broke up with me. I don't want to talk about it."

"If she broke up with you," said Vinnie, "you can still do the janies. You got nothing more to lose. Problem solved."

"I promised I wouldn't," said Reeve.

"Promises to girls you broke up with don't count."

"Yes, they do."

"Reeve. You didn't keep the promises when you *were* going out with her. Why would you decide to be honorable now that you're *not* going out with her?"

Reeve must have used the right tone of voice. When he said again, "No. I'm not doing it any-more," they knew he meant it.

It was not Vinnie who attacked, but Derek. *"You took my hour,"* he said. "I had that hour, Reeve, and I had to give it up."

For the second time that week, Reeve stood in a small, crowded room while people said how much they hated him.

"I had a perfectly good program, Reeve!" Derek was shaking with the kind of rage that wants to wrap itself around something, like a throat. "You took it, and I became nothing but your lead-in. Vinnie put me on the shelf. And did I put a bullet through you or trip you up or do any of the hundred things I could have done to make you fail? No. I didn't. Even I had to admit how good you were. And even if it isn't me doing it, this station has gotten the importance it deserves. I love this station. You're going to take the audience you've built up and throw it away? I'll throw you away first! Don't even think about it, Reeve. You'll be here Tuesday, and you'll do janies, and you'll be back after Thanksgiving, and you'll do your best, too."

•   •   •

So, his resignation hadn't gone that well.

The dorm did not prove to be safe.

Vinnie followed Reeve to his room. He'd called in reinforcements. Visionary Assassins came with him.

Naturally Cordell and Pammy stayed to see what was happening. The room had never been so crowded. When everybody was seated, mostly on the floor, Vinnie closed the door and leaned against it, to prevent Reeve from leaving.

"Visionary Assassins," explained Vinnie, in a new, gentle voice, "has a special club date. Big-name recording companies are sending representatives to hear them play the week after Thanksgiving at Peaches n Crude."

Reeve was genuinely surprised and thrilled for them. "That's wonderful!" he said. "What's the label? When did you find out? Which tape did you send them?"

151

"We need you," said the Assassins, brushing aside detail. "WSCK will announce this week and next week that you're going to do a live janie that night. We'll have lines out the door of Peaches n Crude. Think how impressed the studios will be! They won't know it's for janies and not us. We want a packed house."

Reeve thought of introducing the Assassins at the club. A live audience. He ached, wanting that mike. "No," he said. "I'm not doing janies anymore. Good luck with your club night, and—"

"It could be your chance, too, Reeve," said Vinnie, still in the new, gentle voice.

"The big time," said one of the Assassins. The kid's eyes were glowing, heat produced by the fantasy of the big time.

Reeve's fantasies were just as big. He was in the Little League of radio. He had a chance to make the majors. Stop, he said to himself, stop, stop, stop. "I'm not going into radio, I'm just having fun while I'm getting my degree."

"Come on," said Cordell, "you don't even know what courses you're taking."

"In the really top radio markets," said Vinnie, "they pull in thirty, forty million dollars a year in advertising. You're wasted on a college station that can't take advertising, Reeve. We got plans to spring you from this little station. Make you big-time."

Reeve had never had a close encounter with willpower.

Mostly, he did what he felt like doing.

Okay, senior year in high school he had buckled down to study, so that he could get into college after all. But it had taken no willpower. It had just been the right time for studying.

Reeve made himself think of the Johnsons and the Springs. "No," he said. "You'll pack the club on your own, you don't need me, and I'm done with the janies."

He thought Vinnie would kill him. Vinnie yanked the wooden school-type chair out from underneath Cordell and raised it like a lion-tamer.

"We don't mind filth and roaches, Vinnie," said Cordell, "but we hate blood."

"What do you think college is for?" Vinnie spat at Reeve. "It's for finding a place in the world. We've got a chance at a terrific place. Reeve, you have to do it."

I don't want to be a shock jock, Reeve said to himself, it's a scum career for scum people. Course, I'd fit right in.

He ran his hands over his unshaved face. Maybe he'd grow a beard; hide behind stubble. "No," he said.

Vinnie tried to steady himself by setting the chair down very carefully, centering it on some invisible quadrant. "Reeve, she's not gonna know. You're making this big sacrifice for a girl who won't talk to you anymore. So who cares? You're doing this for somebody who isn't going to give you points."

"Rich and famous," said Pammy, "is always good."

•   •   •

Reeve didn't sleep much that night.

Sleep was one of the surprises of college. The

153

dorm divided between people who never slept, who began partying at midnight and were going strong hours later, and people who slept continually, napping, dozing, sleeping on their bed, sleeping on your bed, sleeping through riots and marathons and ringing phones—Olympic levels of sleep.

Reeve envied both.

He could neither party nor sleep.

He could only lie there.

I'm weak, he thought. I managed to say no to Vinnie and the Assassins, but they'll work on me, and Thanksgiving will be filled with Megan, Todd and Lizzie, who are all better than I am, and Janie will be right next door refusing to talk to me. So I'll get back here feeling low and crummy and Vinnie will tell me how wonderful I am, how they need me, how I matter, and I'll fall for it.

So even quitting the station isn't enough! I have to quit school. Live at home. Work for a while. Maybe next fall go to some college where they don't have a radio station.

He thought of Janie, and Sarah-Charlotte's advice in the gym. Fight or flight. He would never have said, *never,* that he, Reeve Shields, would choose flight.

He wanted to talk to Janie. Nobody knew him better. But she had known the old him; the nice, bland high school him. She didn't want to know the new him.

Neither do I, thought Reeve.

He had the experience of waking up in the morning, so he must have fallen asleep. He tried to remember if he had attended a single class the previous week. Nothing came to mind.

He went to the cafeteria for breakfast. Maybe a nice, wholesome start—bananas, orange juice—would make him a nice, wholesome person. Two pretty girls in heavy sweatshirts walked in as Reeve did.

"Reeve," said one, delighted. "I love your show."

He couldn't help grinning.

She blocked his path to the breakfast line. "What's this rumor I hear that you're quitting the station?"

"It's not a rumor."

"No, Reeve, come on! Our whole floor listens. We've even gotten used to Visionary Assassins. Are they paying you or something?" The girls were bouncing around him, as if he were a star.

"Thanksgiving is such an interruption," said the other girl. "We leave school tomorrow afternoon! You've got to do tonight, anyhow."

Reeve pretended to look at his watch. "I gotta run. You have a great day."

"But are you doing a janie tonight?" they called after him.

He waved, jogged out of the building, and kept jogging. The muscles pulling felt good. His body, at least, was pleased with him. He ran down one Boston street after another, until his unaccustomed calves were aching and the stitch in his side could no longer be ignored.

After so much running, he was starving and made the mistake of going back to the cafeteria, where Derek caught him. Reeve had a loaded tray, was coming down the checkout line with his ID card, had nowhere to set the tray except on a table, and Derek joined him. "You coming tonight?"

155

Reeve began to chew on his food.

"There's the Visionary Assassins club date to push," said Derek mildly, "and we've logged a lot of calls for more janies before vacation."

Any from Hannah? Reeve wanted to ask.

"Why don't you just answer the phones?" suggested Derek. "Or you could study in the hall."

Vinnie and Derek knew perfectly well that Reeve couldn't stand it. His tiny, pathetic willpower would be gone. He'd seize the mike.

So he must not go.

On the other hand, here was his chance to field that hannah call. Everybody who listened knew the janies were Tuesday-Thursday. If there was to be another call, it would be tonight.

Reeve imagined the pause before the woman spoke. The rasping voice.

The heavy copper taste filled his mouth again.

If radio stations pay a lot for a decent jock, he thought, what would they pay for a guy who could draw a kidnapper out of thin air?

The image of himself, on talk shows across the nation, featured morning, evening and postmidnight, glistened like gold.

CHAPTER
FIFTEEN

Reeve's brilliant sister Megan looked solid and stunning.

His more brilliant sister Lizzie looked thin and stunning.

His slightly less brilliant brother, Todd, looked tan, joyful, proud, in love and of course not only stunning, but also equipped now with an equally stunning bride.

Nobody got around to asking Reeve whether he was stunning.

I have a stunning amount of willpower, he said silently, across the turkey and mashed potatoes (for Dad) and sweet potatoes (for Megan) and scalloped potatoes (for Todd) and brown rice (for Lizzie). My willpower has lasted me one entire week.

He gathered his willpower in his bare hands and walked next door to corner Janie in front of her parents.

• • •

The Johnsons had gone to a restaurant for Thanksgiving dinner.

Mrs. Johnson was regal, in very high heels, everything plum-colored: skirt, jacket, stockings. She looked beautiful, in a sixty-year-old way. Mr.

Johnson wore the kind of suit Reeve associated with Wall Street, with a vest and a red bow tie that would have looked ridiculous on Reeve, and a cigar in his pocket. Reeve wanted a cigar conversation. How did they taste? Did Mrs. Johnson allow him to smoke it in the house? Would Mr. Johnson let Reeve try?

Mr. Johnson was laughing. "That's a cigar look," he said. "I know a cigar look when I see one."

"And the answer, Reeve," said Mrs. Johnson, "is no. Absolutely not. You may not begin smoking, you may not share a cigar, and in order to prevent cigar fantasies, you and Janie may go for a ride. Just be back in an hour because we have guests coming over."

"Guests now?" said Reeve. "On Thanksgiving Day, but not for dinner?"

"That's the best kind, the not for dinner kind," said Mrs. Johnson. "They're here for dessert and coffee."

Janie had not said a single word, or looked at Reeve, either. But he had just been handed time alone with her. Thank you, Johnsons.

He turned. He faced her. She was expressionless. He fastened a smile on his face. She got her coat, got her mittens, got her scarf. There was going to be a lot of knitting between him and Janie.

In her driveway, divided from his own by a row of sorry-looking shrubs, Janie said, "I'm going with you only so I don't have to make explanations to my parents." She opened her door, got in and slammed it, before he could touch her or her door.

He drove down the old roads they used to love in

high school: a view, a bridge, a sharp corner where he liked to leave a patch.

Janie said nothing.

In college, when they were apart, she had seemed so distant that she hardly seemed to exist. Now her presence consumed him. "Oh, Janie," he said miserably.

She shrugged.

At the next stop sign, he looked at her. She was crying. "Janie, please don't cry."

"Just drive," she said. "Don't talk to me, don't comfort me, don't do anything but kill time until we can go home. I'm going to tell my parents you have a girlfriend in Boston, the distance was too much, you forgot me. That's the only explanation I can think of for why you're not going to call, fax, e-mail, or Hallmark-card me again. We've broken up."

He actually felt broken.

He had known from the moment Brian called WSCK that this would happen, and yet he had refused to believe it.

It took him a few blocks to put his speech back together. "I don't want to break up, Janie."

She did not bother to respond.

"I'm going to quit college, Janie. It's the only way to keep myself off the radio."

"You loved it that much, selling me? The only way to quit the radio station is to quit college?"

He arranged his thoughts, which was not easy. Being with Janie disarranged every thought. He needed to explain the pressure on him; the anger of his friends; how he could not face that for three and a half more years.

Before he'd thought about it, he had put his hand on her mitten.

She ripped her hand away. "You're nothing but a quitter anyhow, Reeve. Compared to your sisters and your brother, you're nothing. How does it feel to be with them and see that? They're trying to do good in the world, while you're out there trying to destroy it. And then you don't even have the guts to face it."

He wanted to argue with each sentence, but he didn't know how. "I just tried to fill airtime, Janie."

"You could have thought ahead five minutes."

He had thought ahead five minutes. Right up to the next janie.

He wanted to talk about the capital letter, but he could not imagine it. See, I reduced you; once I made you a lowercase letter, it was easy.

He'd put the heat on. Janie snapped it off, as if to prove she was stronger than car fixtures. She was blazing. He found her incredibly attractive. Her hair was flying up, flying out, taking control of the scarf, getting in her mouth, getting in her way.

"Janie," he said, "could you consider my virtues instead of my vices?"

"No." The rage was over, she was just sick of him. "Take us home, Reeve."

"Janie, if I could turn the calendar back, I would. I'd go to football games instead."

"But you didn't, Reeve, and I don't want to talk about what could have happened."

"Janie, listen!" He yanked the car to the side of the road, leaving the signal on. She turned her back on him and looked out her window. "I was weak. I knuckled under. It was like being offered

160

gold. And it *was* gold, Janie. *I was gold.* I never had success before. I never had people treat me like a celebrity. I knew I shouldn't do it. I knew it wasn't me, it was you. Your story, not my voice."

He wanted her to turn. He wanted to see her eyes, wanted this audience, of all his audiences, to be live.

Janie did not move.

• • •

Barbie has Ken, thought Janie, and Ken is great, but Barbie doesn't have an outfit that makes her into a Ken accessory. Barbie has a life. Or actually, dozens of lives.

I was planning to be a Reeve accessory. That way I wouldn't have to have a life. I was going to lie out on the teak deck of our yacht, while he did the sailing. After all, if you run you own life, you might screw up. Like my parents with Hannah. Like Reeve with me.

That's why I don't even want a driver's license. I wanted Reeve to drive.

She was only inches away from Reeve, but he wasn't there; not her Reeve; and she missed him so much that she wept for him. She looked out the side window at the frozen ground and the fallen leaves, instead of across the Jeep at the person pretending to be Reeve.

Who's pretending to be whom? she thought. I'm the only real life person I know who gets two lives and two names. I don't want either of them. I want Reeve, the way I planned for him to be.

• • •

He had primed himself to use that terrible word *rape,* that awful knowledge he'd had, that his talk radio had been the rape of her soul. He could not utter the word. He could not stand the thought of himself in that role.

He said, "Janie, I love you, but I'm not a saint, any more than you are." Out came the words he knew he should never say, just as the wrong words had continually come out on the air. "You were a brat to the Springs, Janie. You're the one who made it so hard for everybody. I admit that I—"

"*I hate you. Don't you compare us.* I was forced into the choices I made. Nobody forced you, Reeve. Don't pretend you're a victim. You *chose* your little golden opportunity. Don't you dare tell me you love me. There is no love in what you did."

He was pressed as hard against his window as she was against hers. "You're right, there was no love in what I did, but I love you anyway."

"I do not love you anyway. Take me home."

He took her home.

When they reached their double driveway, he wanted to hold her in the car by force. *Make* her listen. He stopped himself. It would be proof that not only was he stupid, but he could get stupider.

•   •   •

On Friday Reeve watched from the window when Jodie and Brian pulled up at the Johnsons', stayed an hour, and left with Janie. Exchanging Janie remained something the kids could do fairly easily and the parents could hardly do at all.

His sisters and brother and Heather had gone into New York City for the day. He wished he

162

had gone. He found his parents and came out with it.

"Boston isn't right for me," Reeve told his parents. "I'll finish the semester, and then I thought I'd come home and work for a while. Maybe go back to college next September. I saw an ad in the window at Dairy Mart, and I could probably—"

"You get a job at Dairy Mart," said his father, *"making change for people buying a candy bar, and you might just as well lie down in the driveway and I'll run over you until you're part of the asphalt."*

Reeve stared at his father.

"You think we went through eighteen years of raising you so you could work at a convenience store?"

"Well—"

"Well, we didn't. I don't care how you feel about Boston. You're staying in college!"

Reeve felt as if he had skipped some really important part of life. His parents were mental cases. He had never expected this. In fact, he'd forgotten to think about his parents, he'd been so busy thinking about the janies or Janie and the hannahs or Hannah.

"Are you failing?" shouted his father. *"Are they going to kick you out anyway, is that what this is about?"*

He had no idea whether he was failing. It was a possibility.

"You quit," said Reeve's mother courteously, "and don't come home thinking you'll find free room and board here. You quit college and we're done paying your bills."

Reeve sank back in his chair. He tried to regroup. "Maybe I could transfer to a state university, which would be cheaper, and maybe—"

"You finish your freshman year where you are," said his father.

Reeve wondered what Janie, Jodie and Brian were talking about on the drive to southern New Jersey. Scum Reeve, probably.

The only people who still liked him were people he hadn't met yet.

"Is this about Janie?" his father asked, more calmly. "Are you so stuck on her that you can't be separated?"

He wondered if his father had ever been such a complete jerk that it changed the course of his life and wounded others. "I don't know, Dad," he said finally. "College wasn't what I thought it would be. *I'm* not what I thought I would be."

His mother did not seem to think this was a major issue. "Just try harder then, dear," she told him.

•   •   •

Mr. Spring felt like a teenager.

What pure joy when his oldest child, his beloved Stephen, got off the plane for four whole days at home. So tall now. Such an adult. Stephen was a strong, good person. Too sheltered, yes; Mr. Spring could admit now that he and his wife had overdone the protection angle. But Stephen had rarely failed to give his parents what they needed, and since they needed to see him over Thanksgiving, he had come.

Mr. Spring loved everything about Stephen. He

164

had resigned himself to losing this son when Stephen had left for the West. He knew the burden Stephen planned to leave behind, and he agreed with the decision.

But Stephen had come home grinning and easygoing.

Stephen had hugged his father at the airport, and the hug was long, and was repeated. It was strange to have a son so much taller than he was. Strange to realize that Stephen, if he chose, could grow just as bristly and red a beard.

And the new house, on this first holiday, was fine, too.

Saying good-bye to the cramped split-level was saying good-bye to so much pain.

Back when his baby girl had gone missing, Jonathan Spring had needed to hear his other children in the night; needed to be a thin wall and a whisper away in case they needed him.

That was over.

This fall, he had a sense of youth. He loved his job again, loved the expanse of the new house, loved the huge garage and the workshop and most of all the kitchen, where at last they had enough room for soft drinks to last the week and enough space to sprawl out and enjoy each other.

And when Janie came down to visit, by her own choice, though she was not as happy and easy as her father wanted her to be, still, it was pure thanksgiving.

Thanksgiving without the capital *T*.

Generic everyday wonderful family thanksgiving.

They were together.

CHAPTER
SIXTEEN

Seldom had Reeve found his family more exhausting. Todd expected worship of Heather. Megan expected discussion of her brilliant contributions to computer technology. Lizzie expected admiration of her fabulous new job.

Reeve wished he knew when their planes left.

Sunday breakfast seemed to last even longer than Thanksgiving dinner had.

Todd patted Heather and grinned like an idiot when Heather patted back. Reeve tried to be glad for his brother, falling in love and being happy, but he got sick when he thought how he'd killed it with Janie. Never mind how sick he got when he thought of returning to Boston and fending off Vinnie and Derek.

Reeve retreated to the little den, where the old furniture and the small TV huddled. To his dismay, Lizzie followed.

Reeve had omitted Lizzie from his radio talks; snippy older sisters weren't good talk show material. But Lizzie had been part of the unraveling of the Janie mystery. She had helped make some crucial decisions.

Lizzie came in carrying a glass of ice water and the fruit bowl. Lizzie was very thin; she didn't even

166

eat two grapes in a row. She closed the door firmly. "We have something to talk about, Reeve. It's about Hannah."

Fear lanced him. Did Lizzie know about the janies? But how could she know? She was a lawyer in California.

He did not want Lizzie to despise him.

He sat across from Lizzie, waiting for her to begin.

"As you know, the cult Hannah joined is based in California. Evidence began to appear that drug smuggling was the moneymaker that kept the cult going. My law firm has been involved. I happened to get access to the files."

Reeve felt toasted. "And?"

Lizzie frowned at her brother. She had especially good frowns. "I do not want you to tell Janie."

Not a problem, thought Reeve dizzily. I'll add it to the list of ten thousand things Janie is not going to allow me to tell her anyway.

"The cult," said Lizzie, "kept decent records, considering what a strange mind-set those people had. Among their off-the-wall beliefs was the—"

"Who cares what their commandments were? What about Hannah?" demanded Reeve.

"I found her."

•　•　•

Sunday afternoon, Stephen was flying out of Philadelphia. Mr. Spring drove him to the airport. The family, including Janie, gathered for farewells.

How courteous Stephen was to Janie this time, his hostility laid to rest. He'd smiled hello when Janie, Jodie and Brian hauled in from Connecti-

167

cut. Now, as he and his father left for the airport, Stephen gave Janie an almost-kiss on the cheek. His lips did not touch her. Or maybe she had pulled back. She didn't know. "Good-bye, Stephen," she said. And then, uncertainly, "I'll see you at Christmas."

Stephen actually grinned. "That'd be great, Janie." This time his kiss landed. He got into the driver's seat. College kids didn't get driving time; they had to seize it during vacations.

Her father did not get into the car right away. He frowned slightly at the tires, as if the treads had chosen this particular moment to wear down. "I won't be back from the airport by the time you leave, Janie," he said.

A huge part of Janie grew up.

Because the sentence had nothing to do with airports. He was asking—as Sarah-Charlotte asked questions—without the question. He was asking her to miss him, too.

And I will, she thought. She flung her arms around him. Even though she had not planned the hug, it didn't surprise her that it happened so well and so fast. Dad's hug back did surprise her. It was a grateful hug; a let-my-breath-out-at-last hug. Janie started to say Thank you for having me, but it sounded like a guest speaking, not a daughter, and she heard herself say, "Drive carefully, Dad," and she knew how much older she was. Because that sentence didn't mean cars, either: It meant *Don't you get hurt! I love you. Come home safe.*

Janie and the Springs waved until the car was

168

out of sight. Reeve had accused her of being the brat who'd made this year so hard. *It was true.* Look how they offer themselves, time after time, while I—I pick out the blanket I'm going to hide in.

She followed the rest back indoors.

In one way, the new house was the same as the old: The family gravitated toward the kitchen, coming together as close to the refrigerator as they could get. Reeve had claimed on the air that her Spring parents were just clutter. *Clutter* was a good word for how the Springs lived. Everybody's everything was everywhere. But *they* weren't clutter.

The old tears, last year's tears, heated up behind her eyes. *I'm so sorry,* she thought.

Brian had been assigned dishes. There were a lot after a huge Sunday dinner. (Brendan, of course, was at school. Different sport, same hours.) Brian scraped, rinsed and loaded. Then he filled the sink with the pots and pans and soapy water. When he was done, the dishtowel was soaked. Brian wrung it out over the sink, wrenching his fingers in opposite directions. Then he strangled it the other way, his expression brutal.

"What are you doing?" exclaimed their mother. "Practicing murder?"

Brian blushed. "I don't have a victim yet," he said. He did, of course: Reeve. "Just a style."

"Stop it," said their mother predictably. "Don't talk like that."

My mother, too, thought Janie. I'm here in my kitchen with my mother and my sister and my brother.

How thoroughly she had avoided their love. Stephen grew up, she thought. I wonder if I could ever grow up.

The family room where they sat was directly off the kitchen. Winter sun touched lightly on freshly painted walls. Thin shadows from each square pane of glass crisscrossed the carpet. Mrs. Spring had brought in the geraniums of summer, and pot after pot still put forth cherry-red handfuls of bloom.

For a moment it seemed like a dollhouse to Janie. The doll family was large, as doll families were, because you kept buying more.

She didn't need dolls anymore. She needed a parent. Janie said, "Mom?"

Brian turned from the sink.

Jodie looked up from her term paper.

"Mom, I need to tell you what happened in Boston," said Janie. Her tears rose up like a great and awful fountain, lifting, arching through her, spilling over.

•   •   •

Found her.

Found Hannah.

Reeve's head spun. He felt as if his mind, like a bottle cap, could be screwed right off.

So the voice *had* been Hannah!

Hannah *did* exist.

The worst was about to happen. And the worst not only for Janie's two families, but also for Reeve, because now he could not hide this from Janie. If she had thought him roadkill before, now she would want to shovel him up and dispose of him.

What he had done was very little. Just talk. But the results of what he had done . . .

Reeve felt like an aluminum soda can, caught in a fist, squashed out of shape, all his smooth life turned to knife edges.

We hate you, so it's hate, so shut up and leave.

If you even *liked* me, you would have stopped yourself from doing this.

Don't call me. It hurts me. Stop hurting me.

Oh, God, and the hurt had only just begun.

Reeve tried to find something to cling to, but there was nothing, not in his head, not in this room.

"She's dead," said Lizzie. "The cult file notates her death five years ago."

The dizziness left Reeve slowly, screwing the cap of his brain back down. Dead.

Hannah was dead. Had been dead all along.

So the voice on the radio—the voice had been somebody just like Reeve, wanting to up the ante. Wanting radio time. Wanting to hear herself on a broadcast. Let's have fun, said the voice on the radio, let's not worry about what this could do.

Dead was no threat. Dead was no publicity. It was the best thing for Hannah to be. Not lost, but dead. "Why haven't the Johnsons been notified?" he said.

Lizzie shrugged. "They probably don't know there's a connection yet. Eventually word will filter back to the authorities who were searching for Hannah, and then the information will reach the Johnsons. Don't tell Janie, Reeve. Or anyone else. I know I can trust you."

She knows she can trust me not to tell anybody

171

anything, thought Reeve. Shame flattened his heart, as if Lizzie had run over him with a truck and he really was roadkill. Janie, too, had known she could trust him.

"Why tell me?" he said. He was very tired. What if it showed? What if Lizzie saw through to his untrustworthy core?

"I was so relieved when I found out that I had to share it," said his sister. "Hannah was such a threat. Happiness is so precarious. Hannah alive could have tilted the balance so that neither Janie nor her parents could be happy again."

He was touched that Lizzie, too, had this core: gentle and thoughtful. His radio prayers had been fake. A joke between assassins. This one was real: *Please, God, let my core be something good. Let me not be weak in the center.*

Lizzie nibbled a grape. How could she snack on one grape? Grapes were hardly even food to start with. Abruptly Reeve was hugely hungry. "You're sure about this, Lizzie?" He stood up to go into the kitchen and construct himself a many-layered sandwich. "You're sure you have the right person and Hannah's really dead?"

Lizzie, for whom gentleness was a passing thing, glared at her brother. Information she passed out was flawless. "Hannah was buried in Los Angeles County. Public record."

"It's not somebody pretending to be Hannah?" said Reeve.

"Why would anybody pretend to be that pathetic failure?" snapped Lizzie. "She wasn't even good at being a cult member. Yes, I'm sure it's Hannah and I'm sure she's dead."

• • •

Janie was in the arms of the mother who had not rocked her in more than twelve years. Tears and words fell together. "Oh, Mom, I'm so sorry, Brian and Jodie and I agreed not to tell our parents, we agreed that it was too hard, and it *is* too hard, and I didn't want you to know, because you have *enough* hard things, but my other mother—she isn't strong—she can't take anything more. And I don't know what to do."

It *is* too hard, thought Brian. Much too hard. I'm glad I'm the youngest here and I don't have to pretend I can solve anything.

Mom smoothed Janie's hair. Brian was struck by the motion. His mother was not rocking sixteen-year-old Janie Johnson but three-year-old Jennie Spring. "What happened, honey?" she said, in the warm, round voice of one who will kiss it and make it better.

But Janie was unable to get the words out.

"Not me," said Brian.

So Jodie told. She left out nothing.

Mom's hands continued to soothe, but her face grew harsh. She looked away from Janie's red curls, looked briefly at Jodie and Brian, who shared that hair, and then looked at nothing. Into the terrible past, perhaps, which had just turned active again.

Jodie wrapped up. "And Reeve keeps calling Janie. And he says he's sorry and she should let him explain. Like there's an explanation! Other than the fact that he's slime. He even wants her to forgive him."

173

Their mother said nothing. She just rocked and cuddled.

When Janie was done crying and had straightened up, and the Kleenex box had been passed, and Brian had gotten everybody another Coke, Mrs. Spring finger-combed Janie's curls. "I'm proud of you, honey. You are protecting your mother and father. You know they can't bear any more, so you won't allow it to hit them. You are so strong, Janie. And I am so proud."

The room was quiet. Brian felt the sun on his back. The Coke was cold in his hand. He could hear the tiny *ping* of its bubbles rising and breaking, like their hearts.

"But now what?" said Janie.

It was always the question. *Now what?*

"Janie, to go on in this world, you have to let painful things become history. History has a certain beauty. You can leave things there. Your kidnapping is history. Hannah is history. Those lost twelve years in our family, they're history. I think it's Reeve's turn to be history."

•   •   •

For a moment there, as he wolfed down his turkey on rye, Reeve's life seemed okay again. He could get Janie back, he could—

No.

He could not get Janie back.

Hannah dead did not change that. His voice would still be a voice that hurt.

Janie wasn't a thing that he could go over and get.

If only he could tell her all that he had learned!

174

But she was right not to let him, because he had learned on her, as if she were a computer program, with little graphics of large and small J's.

He still had to stay away from WSCK. Maybe Vinnie was right; maybe he was addicted to the sound of his own voice and had to stay away from radio, like Hannah from the cult, or an alcoholic from bars.

Jamming his hands down into his pockets, Reeve walked into the deep backyard, which was heavy with pine trees; he stirred up cardinals and bluejays.

He wanted to share the great news with somebody: *It wasn't Hannah!*

But nobody else had ever worried. And he had to quit sharing great news. That was what had got him here to start with. Too much sharing.

• • •

Jodie thought about history.

I'm letting Reeve and the radio station dictate to me. I'm letting him decide what college I go to, what city I live in. I have to make Reeve history. Make my own decisions without thinking of him.

She felt released. The future would work after all.

Brian thought about history. History for him was alive. The history of this family would live as long as they did. Could painful things be set aside? Should they? Shouldn't you keep history alive, remembering the bad, not letting it happen again? Remembering the good, struggling to repeat it?

Janie thought about history. Hers included Reeve. She could not bear the thought of discarding him. Yet he, time and again, had discarded her. She knew the shape of the box in which memories of Reeve must be stored in the dark. But I still love him, she thought.

Janie's mother thought of history. Her lost daughter had finally said *us. Mom. Dad.* This lost sister wanted to see Stephen at Christmas. This missing child had at last allowed her to be a mother, and to hug and rock and comfort and kiss.

My baby is home, thought her mother. I am through waiting. I have her back. Only for this weekend, not for this life, but at last, she came to *me.*

The daughter she hardly knew lifted a tear-stained face. "Oh, Mom, I know I shouldn't feel this way, but part of me still loves Reeve."

How beautiful was this child's face. How precious. "Of course you do. He did love you, we all saw that, and you loved back. He gave you strength when you needed it."

"And sold it," Jodie reminded them. "Not because he needed to. Just to show off."

I bet Jodie had tantrums once, thought Janie. I bet she kicked doors shut and ripped her Barbies' heads off.

"Still," said their mother, "you weigh that in. He was cruel to you, Janie, and to us, and it's easy to hate him for that."

Janie could see neither hate nor anger in her mother's eyes, only an expression similar to her father's hug, a let-my-breath-out-at-last look.

"But he was wonderful once," Mrs. Spring said, "and I honor him for that."

Janie touched her mother's bare arm. While

Janie liked a shirt and sweater in November, her mother still wore just a T-shirt. Her skin was warm and tan. Barbies are warm and tan and always the same, thought Janie, but real people are not always the same. They are always, relentlessly, somebody you didn't know they would be.

It was not Reeve she was thinking of. It was herself.

I am Jennie Spring, she thought. I am this woman's child.

"In math," said Jodie darkly, "a plus and a minus equal a zero, so he's a zero, so abandon the creep, Janie."

"But in people," said Janie, "plus and minus are always there. Nobody adds up." In October, she and Sarah Charlotte had had their usual wedding conversation, and it had passed through her mind that if she asked both her fathers to escort her, they'd do it for her—but at what cost?

At what cost, thought Janie, did this mother agree to call me by a different name? At what cost does she refer to the Johnsons as my parents?

Janie's eyes filled again with tears, and Brian, seeing this, thought, She wants a way out. He watched his mother, knowing she would give Janie a way out.

"Or," said Mom softly, "you could forgive him."

"What?" shrieked Jodie. "Mom! The guy's scum. We're not forgiving Reeve."

"Go, Jo!" said Brian, cheerleading.

"You want me to shrug off what he's done," said Janie in disbelief.

"You never shrug," said Janie's mother. "Shrugging means it doesn't matter, and it matters. It matters so much. But forgive, Janie, and you move on."

"Move on where?" cried Janie. "I don't see the next place."

Their mother sighed deeply, and suddenly Brian did not want to be here, did not want to be within miles of this place, wanted to be in good old Colorado with Stephen.

"I had a daughter once," said Mrs. Spring, "who preferred another mother. I did not see how I could forgive a thing like that. Nobody hurt me more. Not even Hannah. But I loved that daughter. So I forgave her."

Jodie cringed.

Brian felt ill.

And Janie whispered, "I'm sorry."

"I know you are. And maybe Reeve is."

"How could I go on loving Reeve?"

"We went on loving you," said her mother.

•   •   •

Brian felt he would really much rather watch television. Jodie went to change clothes before she and Janie set off for Connecticut.

Mrs. Spring and Janie were alone with the fading sun.

An afghan lay on the back of the sofa. Somebody with a poor color eye had crocheted it; the pinks were too purple and the blues were too turquoise. As Janie reached for it, her hand passed over her mother's bare arms. It isn't chilly in here, she thought, I'm not after warmth. Sarah-Charlotte knew the rule: Don't hide, don't run. But I can't learn. Here I am, one more time, trying to wrap myself in a blanket and hide.

"Mom," said Janie. It was a strange feeling, telling the truth. "A mother and a boyfriend are not the same. You can't compare forgiving me with me forgiving Reeve."

"No?"

"No. A mother is going to love her daughter no matter what year, or season, or failure, or trouble. Even if it takes a while."

Her mother found the afghan, put it around both of them. When somebody else wraps a blanket around you, it isn't hiding, it's closeness.

Janie tiptoed near her own failure. "And a daughter," she said shakily, "is going to love her mother no matter what, too. Even if it takes a long, long while. But a boyfriend . . ."

"Boyfriends come and go," agreed her mother. "They aren't blood, they aren't family, they aren't forever."

What if she lived here, in this family, with this mother? Where parents stayed strong and problems had solutions?

"I wasn't sure you *were* family," said Janie. "Right up till this afternoon. When we came in from saying good-bye, all of a sudden, this room— it was my room; and you—you were my mother." With great difficulty she added, "And I knew what I had done to you."

"You came home," said her mother. "That's what you have done for me."

And Janie knew then what she had in common with the Springs. It was not red hair. It was strength.

I'm sure of something, thought Janie. *I know who I am.*

Then her mother grinned and jabbed Janie with an elbow. In this family, the parents often behaved like kids themselves. This was a kid grin. "As for Reeve, if you see him again, and you hate his guts, and you want to light the match that will light the fuse that will blow him up in his car—then forgiveness probably isn't for you."

Janie almost laughed. Not quite, because the hurt was still present. "He's too cute to blow up."

"That's undoubtedly part of the problem. He's paid his way by being so cute. Now he knows he's got a cute voice and a cute radio personality as well. It's going to be hard for Reeve. It's more fun to be cute than to have a conscience."

"How come you're not more mad at him?" said Janie. "I want to drive a spike through his heart."

"I guess, having raised a son that age, I'm more able to forgive stupid, difficult teenage boys. Besides, Reeve may *have* a spike in his heart, even as we speak."

"Good," said Janie. "I hope it hurts." Then she heard the middle of her mother's thought. "What did you have to forgive Stephen for?"

Mom shook her head.

"Aren't you going to tell me?"

"No."

Janie wondered if Stephen could tell her; or if he didn't even know, the way Reeve hadn't known the extent of what he was doing. Maybe you had to get caught in order to know how rotten you were. Maybe sometimes your parents didn't catch you on purpose. They didn't want to know how rotten you were, either.

"Do you think that's all that's wrong with Reeve?" Janie asked. "He's stupid and difficult and a teenager? Or do you think he's worthless and disgusting and we should blow him up in his car?"

"I think we should save the car," said Jodie, walking in.

They laughed, and Janie loved them, and she said, "I'm sorry I was such a brat last year."

Her mother held her tight, kissing cheek and throat and hair, the way parents did when you weren't run over by a train after all. She did not pretend that Janie had not been a brat. "Be strong for your parents," she said softly. "Make me proud."

●　　●　　●

It was dark and very late when they got to Janie's.

The shared driveway was full of Reeve's family hugging good bye. Suitcases were being loaded, instructions given, promises to be back for Christmas Eve. Maybe in the chaos, Janie could sneak inside without—

"Yo, Janie!" shouted Todd. "Come over and meet my fiancée, Heather!"

"I'm out of here," said Jodie.

"No, you can't, my parents will be very upset, Jodie, please, don't drive away, come on in and—"

"Bye," said Jodie. "You're on your own. See you at Christmas." Her sister blew a kiss, backed right out and took right off. Some ally, thought Janie.

Todd hauled her around the bushes and pre-

181

sented Heather. "Hi, Heather," said Janie. "Welcome to Connecticut." She tried not to see the rest of the family; she tried not to find out where Reeve stood, and what his expression was, and what clothes he had on.

"Janie! Kisses!" said Lizzie, who preferred to discuss these rather than bestow them.

"We're just taking off," said Megan. "See you at Christmas, Janie!"

And they were gone, and Mrs. Shields went indoors and Janie was standing on the driveway with Reeve. The light from the houses did not reach them. The dark swirled around them like wind.

Shadows took Reeve's face and kept it. He could have been a stranger. Janie stared, trying to see the boy she had known. Reeve flinched and looked away. Twice he took a breath, preparing to speak, and twice wet his lips instead.

He needs a mike for courage, she thought. Oh, Reeve!

Her heart went out to him. She, Janie, had found her strength. Reeve—poor Reeve—had found his weakness.

Long ago, when Janie had decided on one family over the other, a cop had said to grieving, raging Stephen and Jodie: "You got a family that loves you and Jennie's got a family that loves her. What else is there?"

What else is there? thought Janie, as Reeve struggled with speech. Well, there's hurt, and deceit, and selfishness. And then, I guess, if there's any hope of any love anywhere, there has to be the chance to try again.

I don't need a blanket or a hiding place. I can make it with or without an ally. I am a Spring.

"Let's talk, Reeve," she said. She held out her hand, and he took it.

ABOUT THE AUTHOR

Caroline B. Cooney is the author of many novels, including *Driver's Ed* (an ALA Best Book for Young Adults, an ALA Quick Pick for Young Adults, and a *Booklist* Editors' Choice), *The Face on the Milk Carton* (an IRA-CBC Children's Choice Book), its companion *Whatever Happened to Janie?* (an ALA Best Book for Young Adults), *Among Friends, Camp Girl-Meets-Boy, Camp Reunion, Family Reunion, Don't Blame the Music* (an ALA Best Book for Young Adults), *Twenty Pageants Later,* and *Operation: Homefront.* She is also the author of the time travel romance *Both Sides of Time* and its companion *Out of Time.* She lives in Westbrook, Connecticut.

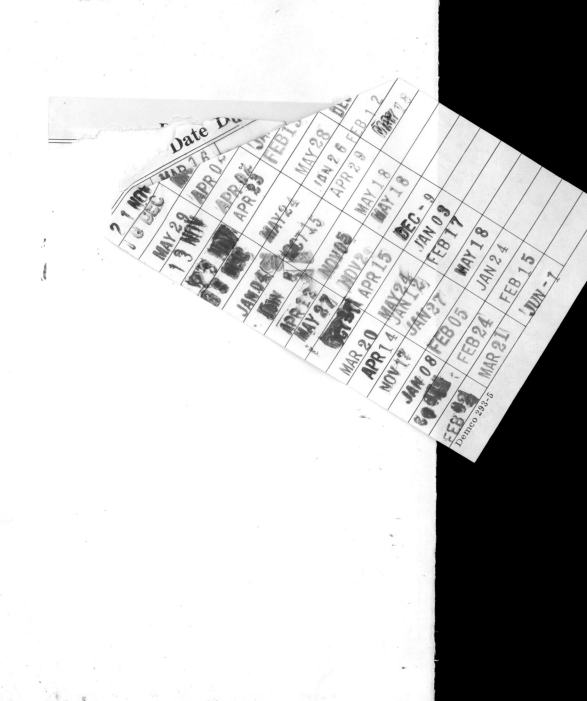